ARIZONA LAW

Expecting to become the mistress of a great ranch, Sylvia Carfax travels from her luxurious New Orleans home to Arizona. She is dismayed to find herself in an impoverished, backwoods spread, run by her potential husband Neil and his tough mother, Ma Grantham. Before Sylvia can return home, she and the Granthams are caught up in the villainous scheming of the suavely attractive Carl Naylor. Unless the ladylike Sylvia can adapt to the dog-eat-dog lifestyle of the Wild West, she is destined to die horribly at the hands of Naylor . . .

CONRAD G. HOLT

ARIZONA LAW

Complete and Unabridged

LINFORD
Leicester

First published in Great Britain in 2004 by
Robert Hale Limited
London

First Linford Edition
published 2005
by arrangement with
Robert Hale Limited
London

British Library CIP Data

Holt, Conrad G.
  Arizona law.—Large print ed.—
Linford western library
1. Western stories
2. Large type books
I. Title
823.9′14 [F]

ISBN 1–84395–805–8

Published by
F. A. Thorpe (Publishing)
Anstey, Leicestershire

Set by Words & Graphics Ltd.
Anstey, Leicestershire
Printed and bound in Great Britain by
T. J. International Ltd., Padstow, Cornwall

This book is printed on acid-free paper

To my Mother

1

Deception

'My ticket?' Sylvia Carfax frowned, dived a hand into her costly bag, and handed over a roll of paper to the grizzled, elderly man in a faded uniform. The man inspected the ticket, nodded, and stood aside.

Sylvia remained where she was, gazing in distaste at the dusty emptiness outside the rail halt, and the huddled mass of wooden dwellings of the small Western town.

'Is there any transport I can get?' she asked, and the stationmaster stared at her in surprise.

'Y'mean a stage or a buckboard, miss?'

'I mean anything on wheels capable of carrying me!' Sylvia was becoming very hot and irritated. 'Somebody from the Blue Circle ranch was supposed to meet me here, and they haven't turned up. I've no idea where the place is, either — '

'Blue Circle, huh? Y'mean Neil Grantham's spread?'

'Certainly I do. There must be *some* way to get myself there and send for my trunk later! I don't understand this. Neil is a very wealthy man with a big ranch . . . '

'First I heard of him bein' wealthy,' the stationmaster commented, scratching his head. 'An' I guess there's only one way to get there if he don't come — take a hoss, or walk it.'

'I can ride a horse easily enough. Have you one I could hire?'

'Nope. I was only making suggestions.'

Sylvia glared. 'And some good they are! How far is it if I decide to walk?'

'About ten miles, I reckon. You go straight down the main street there, follow it to the end, and just keep on

2

going. The Blue Circle's ten miles down the trail.'

To Sylvia's chagrin, the stationmaster turned into a wooden structure like an overgrown sentry box and slammed the door — presumably to attend to his railroad duties. Sylvia muttered an unladylike remark under her breath, then settled disconsolately on her cabin trunk and looked around her.

At her back was the railroad track; to either side was a tangled wilderness of wooden sleepers and small ramshackle buildings that comprised the 'station' — and ahead of her the absurd high street passing through the small town of Arrowhead Bend. Looming in the background were the Pinga mountains, the oppressive sun beginning to dip towards the jagged peaks with the coming of evening.

Sylvia certainly had no intention of walking ten miles, and there was the baffling problem of how to take her cabin trunk with her as well as her suitcase. So she lighted a cigarette and sat smoking it, waiting for something to happen. Neil knew when her train was due, so surely he must come soon?

Time passed. Irritably she flung the stub away. She was hungry and thirsty, as well as weary from her long train journey and uncomfortable slumbers in a sleeping-berth. Fishing a compact from her handbag she went to work to patch up the rouge and lipstick, which the heat had dried.

Then she gave a start. Through the mirror of the compact she had just become aware of a terrifying figure watching over her shoulder. The man had a huge beaked nose, high cheek-bones, a lean jaw and coppery-red skin. Jet-black hair was drawn back from a rather low forehead and fastened at the back of his head. He was staring at her unwaveringly with sloe-black eyes.

Frightened, the girl dropped her compact. The silent figure immediately retrieved it for her, handing it back with a sinewy red hand. She saw that he was dressed in a flannel shirt and belted tweed trousers, and recognized him as an Indian. From her sitting position, he seemed to be enormous — and was in fact six-feet-five tall.

'Don't you *dare* touch me!' she whispered.

The Indian ignored her and heaved the cabin trunk on to one broad shoulder, then with his other hand he grasped her suitcase. He began to stride away through the station's gateway.

Sylvia suddenly came to life. 'Hey, come back! Those are my things — !'

Racing after him through the gateway she saw that a wagon and team was standing just outside. Having finished heaving the suitcase and trunk into the rear of it, the Indian turned and motioned to the wooden driving-seat.

Sylvia was convinced that she was about to be kidnapped. She swung round, with the intention of getting help from the stationmaster — but she had no chance to reach his shack.

In three lithe bounds the Indian

reached her, his powerful hands clamping on her shoulders. She was spun round and swept off her feet. Gasping with alarm, she found herself swung through the air and dumped on the wagon seat. Then the Indian leapt up beside her, whipped the two horses, and set the wagon hurtling down the main street in a cloud of dust.

Sylvia hung on frantically, clutching the small metal rail around the seat edge, as the wind buffeted around her, whipping her skirt savagely and flinging dust into her face.

'Where are you taking me?' Sylvia released one hand from the rail to pound ineffectively on the Indian's sinewy arm. 'Let me *down*!'

The man took no notice, and kept on driving. Sylvia looked in alarm about her as the town of Arrowhead Bend was left behind and the wagon, jolting along the rutted track, went on its way down the trail, bordered on either side by rolling pastures.

Realizing that to try and jump for it

would likely mean a broken leg, Sylvia abandoned the idea. Then she fell to wondering if broken legs could be any worse than maybe being scalped, or held as a captive plaything in some Indian settlement.

At length, through dust-gritted eyes she caught a glimpse of a lone rider ahead. He was speeding towards them in the long bars of evening sunlight. As he came into nearer focus, she saw that he was mounted on a powerful sorrel — and there was something familiar about those broad shoulders and square-cut face under his big sombrero.

'Neil!' she yelled hoarsely. 'Neil, darling!'

As the wagon drew up with a squeaking of brakes, Sylvia threw herself out of the wagon seat and grabbed at the horseman. Unprepared for it he fell sideways out of the saddle, struggling in the dust with the girl on top of him.

'Gosh, Syl, you don't forget to give a feller a greeting!' Neil Grantham laughed, as he disentangled himself and helped the girl to her feet. He hugged and kissed her, then gave her a sharp glance.

'Say, honey, what's wrong? You seem — frightened.'

'That — that horrible creature on the wagon!' Sylvia pointed to the silent Indian still on the driving seat. 'He kidnapped me! Thank heavens you rescued me! He was taking me to his wigwam or something . . . '

Neil stared at her for a moment, then doubled up in helpless laughter. Sylvia watched his performance in cold disapproval.

'What's so amusing?'

'It's my fault entirely,' Neil apologized, his mirth subsiding. 'This chap is perfectly harmless — in fact, he's my servant and right-hand man. His name's Fleeting Cloud — Fleet for short. He's been with me for years and I couldn't do without him.'

Sylvia gazed up at the immobile redskin and then back to Neil. 'Why on earth couldn't he have said so? I was scared out of my wits!'

'I'm afraid he's been dumb since childhood,' Neil explained. 'But he can hear all right, so if ever you need him just yell out and he'll turn up out of a clear sky.'

'I see.' Sylvia looked at the waiting Indian and the impatient horses, then turned her attention back to Neil and smiled.

'You look handsome in that black shirt and pants, and the orange kerchief and fancy boots,' she murmured. 'A real man of the West. I often wondered on my way here if you'd look as — as you do.'

Neil grinned as she continued her appraisal. He was bronzed, with a cleanly lined jaw and dark-blue eyes. The big sombrero hid his hair but Sylvia knew well enough that it was black and waved.

'It's over a year since we met in New Orleans,' he said at length. 'You look exactly the same — the girl I fell in love with. You don't know what it means to have you come out here like this and join me . . . And I'm sorry I was late meeting you. I had a business deal at the last moment, so I dispatched Fleeting Cloud to attend to you. I should have realized you're a total stranger around here and that he might scare you.'

'Business deal?' Sylvia repeated, her eyes brightening. 'A profitable one?'

'Yes . . . Well, sort of,' Neil replied uneasily; then before Sylvia could pursue the topic he reached out and whisked her up to the driving-seat beside Fleeting Cloud.

'I'll ride alongside,' he said, swinging into the saddle of his sorrel, and at that the Indian cracked his whip and set the wagon moving. Sylvia relaxed, now able to appreciate the landscape through which they were passing. She appreciated too the scented air, as the evening breeze, already chilling with the coming of night, carried with it the aroma of wild sweet-pea, whispering bells, and primroses.

Stretching as far as she could see to the mountains were wild verbena and purple hyptis, slashed here and there with coloured rock lichens. Out beyond these fields were the scarlet and orange patchworks of ocotillo and opuntias. Turning in the opposite direction away from the mountains, Sylvia saw fields of yellow brittle-bush, and beyond them in the great expanse of mesa and desert, were the endless wastes of tall yuccas with their clusters of snow-white bloom.

'It's marvellous,' Sylvia whispered, glancing at Neil where he rode below her at the side of the wagon. 'I've never seen anything quite like it.'

'That's because you're city-bred,' he told her. 'In time you'll forget the grime of cities, and become a part of this. Same as Ma and myself, and everyone around here.'

Sylvia contemplated the dark blue dome of heaven. The sun had vanished behind the mountain peaks, edging their saw-teeth with brilliant amber.

'The ranch far?' she asked presently, looking around her.

'Oh, 'bout five more miles, mebbe. You can't see it yet.'

'I'm been looking forward to it, Neil, ever since I left New Orleans. It must be wonderful to be so prosperous in so glorious a country . . . ' Sylvia paused and then half laughed to herself. 'The stationmaster said a strange thing — that you *weren't* prosperous! How utterly ridiculous! You even have a servant — this Indian chap here. In my mind's eye I can just picture the Blue Circle with its four thousand cattle. You did say four thousand, didn't you?'

'Uh-huh,' Neil assented. 'Not that many now though. I've sold quite a few . . . ' Sylvia nodded and looked ahead eagerly, failing to notice the suddenly troubled expression on Neil's face.

Three miles slipped by, then as they rounded a sharp bend and in the midst of the deepening twilight there suddenly loomed a solitary ranch. Sylvia studied it and frowned.

It was not particularly large. There was a ranch house — a sprawling wooden bungalow of moderate dimensions — a few scattered outhouses, a big barn fenced around with wire, and a single corral enclosed by thorny ocotillo bushes, the lopsided gateway firmly secured. Inside were little more than three dozen steers, blatting uneasily at intervals.

'Whose place is that?' Sylvia asked as they came closer.

'Mine,' Neil answered, his voice low.

'You're joking! That little shack and outhouses there *can't* be the huge ranch that you talked about ... Why, this place is just a dump!' Anger thickened the girl's voice. 'What in the world possessed you to lie to me in that fashion?'

Neil compressed his lips, and remained silent.

Reaching the open gateway of the

yard, the Indian drove the wagon through it and then brought the vehicle to a jerking halt outside the ranch house veranda. Sylvia studied the log-walled structure in angry silence, her eyes travelling to the screen-door, the tiny windows, and then the steps leading up to the porch. She glared at Neil as he stood just below the wagon, waiting to help her down.

'Tell me this is a joke,' she said.

'No joke, honey — this is the Blue Circle.' Neil looked at her earnestly in the dying light. 'If you'll only give me a chance I can explain. Let me show you inside, and we can talk things over.'

Because there was nothing else she could do Sylvia allowed herself to be lifted down gently and set on her feet, then Neil glanced up at the redskin.

'Bring in the luggage, Fleet,' he instructed. The Indian nodded and climbed into the back of the wagon.

Neil led the way up the steps and then tugged open the screen-door. In tight-lipped silence Sylvia followed him through a small, gloomy hall into a big living-room, indistinguishable as night suddenly snapped down.

Sylvia waited. A match scraped and flared, then twin oil lamps on the table came into life. This main living-room was fairly large, its furniture comprising a big hardwood table with the oil-lamps in the centre. Against one wall was a bookcase-bureau, the lower desk portion being open and revealing a jumble of papers and ledgers.

For the rest there were chairs, a rough-looking sideboard with a mirror badly in need of resilvering; and a rocking-chair by the window with an archaic antimacassar draped over its back. The walls of the room were seasoned logs, the chinks stopped with red clay. The bare wooden floor was relieved by coconut-matting and a worn skin rug near the big stone fireplace, where logs and thin wood were arranged in the grate.

She was still considering it when

Neal came forward and set the mass on fire. The chill of the room began to soften somewhat as the flames crackled noisily.

'We seem to be alone in the place,' Sylvia said frostily. 'I suppose the story about your grey-haired old mother was a pack of lies, too?'

'Ma will be coming in soon.' Neil's voice was troubled and apologetic. 'She's gone over to Nathan's Cleft to see a friend. Everything is quite ethical,' he insisted. 'Fleeting Cloud lives here too. He'll be busy right now fixing up a meal for us . . . Mebbe you'd like to freshen up, whilst we're waiting?'

'Is it possible to do so in this — cowshed? Or am I supposed to jump head first into a bucket of water?'

His expression chastened, Neil said, 'I'll show you to your room,' and tried to take her arm. She snatched it free. He shrugged, and then led the way from the room, across the narrow strip of hall, at the far end of which, in the small kitchen, the redskin was visible in the midst of lamplight preparing something on a heating stove — and so to another door.

Sylvia stepped into a room and waited as the oil lamp was lit. The room smelled of newly-aired linen. A bed was by the window, a shabby-looking dresser alongside. Across one corner a length of cretonne had been slung to create a hanging wardrobe. Everywhere she looked there seemed to be some object or other that offended her refined senses.

'Get out!' Sylvia snapped abruptly. 'Isn't it enough that you had to tell lies without humiliating me further by giving me a — a den like this to sleep in? I might just as well be serving time, or something! Go on — get out and leave me alone!'

She flung up her hands and pushed Neil savagely through the door. Unprepared for the shove he stumbled back into the hall. Sylvia slammed the door on him. Then, her vision blurred by sudden tears, she flung herself face downward on the bed and battered at the counterpane with her fists.

Her excess of emotion subsiding by slow degrees, she got up from the bed and stared at her reflection in the dresser mirror.

'You blithering idiot!' she whispered. 'You poor, benighted, blithering idiot! You fell for everything that was handed to you and travelled a thousand miles — to this!'

In sudden fury she flung her hat in a corner, followed by her jacket and blouse. Her eyes brimming, she turned to the cabin trunk and suitcase, which Fleeting Cloud had placed in another corner of the room.

2

Ma Grantham Intervenes

Sylvia emerged again from the room and found her way into the big living-quarters. A white cloth had been laid across the hardwood table now and places set for three. Neil was the only one present, moodily playing with a table knife, but the instant he became aware of the girl he was on his feet, smiling.

'Syl, I want to explain — '

'I'm not interested,' she interrupted. 'I'm going to have a meal, stay the night, and then tomorrow I'm setting off for home again.'

'But damn it, you can't leave!' Neil looked at her helplessly.

'Why not? We're not engaged yet — thank heaven! I've no intention of staying in a primitive hole like this

— and most certainly I'd never marry you after the way you've deceived me. Cattle baron!' Sylvia finished sourly. 'At least you've got imagination, if nothing else.'

Neil shifted uncomfortably and it seemed to Sylvia that he had never seemed so big and awkward. Indoors, his six foot three and broad shoulders seemed incredibly huge. There was an awkward silence.

'Well?' Sylvia asked presently, raising a delicately lined eyebrow. 'Do we have something to eat, or don't we? The last meal I had was on the train!'

'Sorry. I guess your reaction to this place has sort of made me forget everything else for the moment.' He settled her in one of the chairs at the table, and then shouted for Fleeting Cloud.

In a moment or two the redskin appeared with his customary utter silence, soft moccasins on his feet. Sylvia watched him uneasily, still unable to rid herself of the conviction that he might suddenly flash a knife on her. Certainly he had one: she could see it in the sheath on his pants belt.

He doled out something from the vegetable dishes on to plates and presently Sylvia found her nostrils twitching over a steamy conglomeration that had been placed before her. She recognized potatoes in the heaped-up mass — but the rest was an enigma.

Neil pushed over a monstrous loaf on a wooden trencher, a big bread-saw beside it.

'It's stew,' he said, catching her look. 'Real good stuff from my very best beef.'

'I loathe stew,' Sylvia stated. 'And the thought of it having come from those horrible, smelly cattle of yours is revolting!' She pushed the plate aside. 'Haven't you got an egg, or a piece of cheese, or something I can understand?'

'Yeah, sure thing, but — honest, honey, I thought you'd like a hot meal. It's delicious: try it.'

'I prefer an egg!' Sylvia snapped. 'Boiled four minutes so it isn't all runny and messy!'

Neil shrugged and glanced at the redskin who was standing imperturbably by the doorway.

'You heard, Fleet,' he said briefly. 'Fix a four-minute egg for the lady.'

Fleeting Cloud departed and Neil fell to eating avidly as Sylvia looked at him across the table.

'I suppose there's something to drink?' she asked miserably.

'Sure there is!' Neil turned to a coffee jug on a stand.

'No tea?' Sylvia asked, sighing. 'I hate coffee because it gives me indigestion.' Neil paused, holding a cup half-filled with black, steaming liquid. He gave a wry smile. 'Sorry, honey. Around here it's considered a bit lily-white to be a tea-drinker. I know they drink it in the towns and cities, but right here we're back o' beyond. It's coffee or nothing.'

Sylvia looked at the half-filled coffee cup, then drew it towards her. She flooded it with milk, added plenty of sugar, and drank it slowly with her eyes tightly shut. Neil shook his head to himself and went on eating.

Abruptly, so suddenly she nearly upset the coffee cup, Sylvia found Fleeting Cloud at her side, lowering an egg in its cup, placed exactly in the centre of a plate.

'Don't hover like that!' she snapped, colouring. The redskin paused and looked at her woodenly. 'It gives me the jumps the state my nerves are in!'

Silence. The redskin glided backwards into the shadows. Then Sylvia cracked the egg viciously and inspected the interior. It was freshly laid and perfectly cooked. She buttered the loaf, and began to cut wafer-thin slices. With a contemptuous glance at Neil, she began to peck and pick her way through a series of egg sandwiches.

When she had finished she reset the make-up on her lips, tugged out a cigarette from her case and lighted it. Silently, smoke drifting from her nostrils, she contemplated the dregs in the coffee cup.

'Better now?' Neil asked her quietly. His own meal also finished, he was rolling a cigarette deftly between finger and thumb.

'Bit less hungry, certainly,' she admitted — and reopening the cigarette case she proffered it.

'No thanks, Syl. Prefer my own, not cissy stuff.'

Sylvia snapped the case shut and slapped it down hard on the tabletop. Then after thinking for a moment or two she said deliberately:

'Obviously, Neil, we have to put an end to this farce. My father is one of the richest men in New Orleans: you know full well the kind of surroundings to which I'm accustomed — and these are impossible. Besides, I can't forgive — or forget — the fact that you lied to me!'

'Yeah,' Neil mused. 'I guess I did.'

Sylvia's eyes pinned him for a moment as he moodily studied his cigarette; then she said: 'When you came to New Orleans to see your uncle last year, I thought it was fate that we met accidentally — and I must say you acted like a hero when you saved me when my horse bolted. In the days that followed, when we got to know each other, you told me you had a huge ranch here in Arizona, with four thousand head of cattle. Remember?'

Neil nodded miserably, lips compressed.

'You also said you were still building it up, and on the way to becoming the most influential man in the district. You asked me to wait until you'd achieved your goal, then you would send for me. I swallowed it all and ever since then I've believed everything you told me in your letters, waiting for the day when you would send for me as you'd promised. When you did send I came — eagerly, because I was looking forward to it. And *this* is what I find! One stage removed from a barn, a dumb redskin for a servant, food that wouldn't pass even in the cheapest, low-down restaurant in the city, and a non-existent mother! Do you realize that I — '

She broke off at a sudden violent bang from the hall. Neil glanced up and said:

'Here's Ma now, I guess. She always bangs the door.'

Sylvia turned in wonder, listening to a powerful voice from the darkness of the hall. 'Hey there, Fleet, quit moonin' around, can't you, an' put the buck-board in the stable! Don't expect me to go gaddin' about with a blasted wagon at my age, do you? Git the hell to work!'

The Indian travelled swiftly into the hall, and then Ma Grantham came into the living-room. A large, square-built woman, she was dressed in a loud check skirt, elastic-sided boots and white stockings, and wearing a pale-pink blouse which enhanced the floppiness of her bosom. She had hardly any neck; her face was perfectly round with red-apple cheeks — strong white teeth grinning in welcome — and a turned-up nose. She wore no hat, and her grey hair was drawn back in a tight bun.

'Howdy, son,' she greeted, flinging aside a hideous plaid over-jacket; then catching sight of Sylvia she regarded her in something close to amazement. Her horny hands clamped on to her ample hips as she gazed. Then she lumbered forward and began to swing Sylvia's right arm up and down fiercely.

'Mighty glad t'see you, gal! Neil's told me plenty 'bout you, I guess, but it didn't add up to anythin' like the real thing . . . ' The woman stood back a little and considered Sylvia critically.

'Yes, *sir*!' she declared finally. 'With the paint off your face I reckon you'd be durned purty. Paint's only for buildings an' barns to my way of thinkin'. It sure ain't the stuff to plaster your pan with.'

'Pan?' Sylvia repeated vaguely. 'Who's talking about pans?'

'Nice voice, too,' Ma Grantham

decided. 'Kinda gentle-like — not like mine,' she yelled, 'with rocks in it. 'Corncrake Milly' they used to call me. Hell's jangling bells, gal, but there ain't no need for the paint on that pan of yourn when God's given you good features. Insult to the Almighty, I calls it.'

Sylvia just blinked, beyond all speech.

'I suppose she can please herself, Ma,' Neil ventured. 'After all, Syl's a city girl, and they use a lot of make-up — '

'I says what I thinks, son.' Ma Grantham sat down at the third place and gave the table a resounding bang with her clenched fist. 'Are you dead on your feet out there, Fleet?' she bawled. 'How's 'bout feedin' this old woman?'

The redskin appeared silently, a hot plate held in a cloth, which he set before her. He ladled out the stew deliberately and the old woman gave a cackle.

'Ain't nothin' like the smell of this!' Ma declared.

'I'm inclined to agree with you,' Sylvia muttered ambiguously. 'I don't like stew,' she added, as Ma gave her a sharp glance. 'I had an egg.'

'Just *one* egg?' Ma Grantham said incredulously. 'Snakes alive! What kind of a meal is that for a gal with flesh on her limbs?'

Since Sylvia did not pursue the subject Ma shrugged and began her meal. Sylvia went on smoking deliberately. Neil shifted his position, looking uneasily at the two women.

'Syl isn't staying, Ma,' he said awkwardly. Ma Grantham lowered the chunk of bread she was holding and looked at Sylvia in sharp enquiry.

'An' why in heck not?' she demanded.

'Because I've been deceived ... ' Sylvia crushed out her cigarette stub in the saucer of her coffee cup. 'I was led by Neil to believe that I was coming to a magnificent ranch with four thousand cattle. Instead I find this.'

'It's a roof, ain't it? Neil's the right sort of man for a husband. What children you have'll be strong and tough — like him. What more d'you want, gal, than a man, a roof, an' kids?'

'I want what I was led to believe I would have. And I don't like a man who lies.'

Ma frowned. 'I'll tell you the reason why he lied. It was because if he hadn't, knowin' the classy dame you are, he knew you'd never come out here to join him. He loved you enough — an' still does — to lie about things to make sure of gettin' you.'

'Ma you don't have to be so blunt about everything,' Neil protested. 'I was going to tell Syl in my own way — '

'I reckon you wasn't,' his mother interrupted flatly. 'I can see in your eyes that you're plumb scared of the gal, and — '

'If you don't mind,' Sylvia interposed, rising, 'I think I'll turn in. I'm dreadfully tired after all the travelling

I've done, and I have to be on my way again tomorrow. Goodnight, Mrs Grantham. Neil.'

'Call me 'Ma', gal! Most folks around here do.'

Sylvia only smiled faintly in response and left the living-room, aware that as she went Neil had got clumsily to his feet and wished her goodnight. When she arrived in her room she closed and bolted the door, lit the lamp and then sat down on the edge of the bed to think. For quite a while she could not make up her mind whether or not to weep with disappointment.

At last she lit another cigarette and dragged at it slowly. The meal, small though it had been, had fortified her somewhat and she was not quite so ready to burst into tears as she had been earlier. She mused on what Ma Grantham had said — that Neil had only lied to make sure of getting her out here.

Because of those lies she had turned her back on her luxurious city house in

New Orleans and the smart set there. She'd thought to be the wife of a wealthy American rancher and cattle baron. Instead she had this — the half-shy young man and his loud-voiced rough diamond of a mother, with the silent, enigmatic redskin in the background.

It would not be easy to return home to New Orleans, either. Her father, bitter at the idea of her making her life in another state, had done the thing properly and as good as disowned her.

Sylvia sighed, got to her feet, and went over to the window. The moon had risen and the curtains were drawn back. She cupped her hand about the chimney lamp, blew out the flame, and gazed on the silent glory of the night. The monstrous bulk of the mountain range had foundered into a greater darkness, cutting jagged caverns out of the deep-violet sky. The mountain crags seemed to scrape the glittering stars. The moon hung low down in the sky, its face orange-tinted with intervening mist, but its rays were bright enough to pick out the tranquil landscape.

She was about to undress when there was a knock on the door.

'Who is it?' she asked uncertainly.

'It's Ma, gal. Can I have a word with you?'

Puzzled, Sylvia drew back the bolt, and opened the door slightly. Immediately Ma Grantham pushed through into the room. Even though she had been expecting her, Sylvia gave a start as she looked at her visitor.

She stood square and massive in a flannel dressing-gown, and was holding a lighted lamp shoulder-high. Its rays were cast on her round face and the pins and papers in her grey hair.

'Close the door, gal. I don't want Neil to know I came to see you.'

As Sylvia complied, Ma moved to a chair and sat down, placing the lamp on the dresser.

'Gal, I don't want to preach to you because I know it won't get through to a high-spirited woman like you. Many's the steer I've broken in the hard way, but I guess I can't treat a filly like you as though you was cattle. I think you oughta know, though, that if you walk out on my boy it'll break his heart.'

Sylvia was silent, her face expressionless. Ma eyed her and went on deliberately:

'He's been countin' for over a year now on you comin' out here to wed him — an' he's worked and slaved getting a bit o'money together to make the marriage possible. Sure, he lied to you — but only because he loves you, which is as good an excuse as any, I reckon. I guess it's the only lie he ever told. I'm not a-pleadin' with you because that ain't my way. I'm just askin' straight — don't walk out on him.'

'I don't think you appreciate my position, Ma,' Sylvia said slowly. 'I'm used to luxury! My father is in the shipping business and one of the richest men in New Orleans. He raised violent objections to my coming out here, even threatening to disown me. I'll have a hard job talking him round when I land home again. I know now he was quite right in his views. Back home I'm used to clothes, money, lots of society friends and city life . . . '

'All of which you were prepared to give up for my son,' Ma pointed out.

'Yes, but only because I expected him to be influential and wealthy, not living in a glorified barn surrounded by coyotes or — ' The girl broke off abruptly as there suddenly came an appalling sound — a long drawn-out wailing from somewhere not far away outside, as though some animal were caught in a trap. She rushed to the window and peered outside, failing to notice the look of amusement on Ma's face.

'Ma! It's an intruder about to attack the ranch!' The words came jerking out as Sylvia saw a stealthy figure creeping across the dim yard towards the corral. The moonlight caught something in the man's hand — a long, thin gleaming line.

'He's carrying a rifle!' Sylvia cried in alarm, swinging round. 'We've got to get Neil!' To her astonishment, Ma started laughing.

'For land's sake, gal, simmer down! There's nothin' to be worryin' about. That's just Fleeting Cloud on the prowl for them coyotes. That wailin' came from one of 'em. They attack the cattle at night sometimes and Fleet does his best to trap them or shoot them down, otherwise they might cause the whale of a lot of damage.'

'But . . . ' Sylvia blinked sleepily. 'Doesn't that horrible redskin ever go to sleep?'

'Only catnaps,' Ma said. 'But he gets in as many hours as you or me in small doses, so's he can stay awake at night. Some nights you might find him ways up on yonder mountains doin' some kind of ritual all his own. Ain't our business. Mebbe dadblamed queer, but every man to his fancy, I guess.'

'Something else I didn't know about.'

Sylvia smiled ruefully.

'Listen, gal, there's a lot about this spread of ours y'don't know yet,' Ma said, more quietly than usual. 'I'll leave you now to get some shut-eye. Guess I've said my piece. But there's just one thing more I need to do . . .'

To Sylvia's astonishment, she found her arms were being gripped tightly; then her body was slapped gently but firmly all over by Ma's big hands.

'You'll do,' Ma decided. Then as Sylvia stared at her blankly she went on:

'Y'say you're not built for this region, gal — but you're wrong. You've plenty of strength in that body! Bit flabby from not bein' exercised, I guess, but you'll soon lose that around here. You can cut out that smokin' an' the paint job on your face an' then you'll be as strong a gal as ever sat astride a cayuse. You'll see! Just think it over, that's all! Good night, gal!'

Silently Ma's shadowy bulk crossed the room; then she was gone and there was the click of the door-latch.

Sylvia smiled to herself, then undressed and got into the bed, which she found unexpectedly comfortable, unless it was that her travelling was catching up on her. Within a few minutes sleep suddenly enveloped her and her next conscious realization was of lying flat on her back, arms thrown wide, and blinding sunlight pouring into her face. To her ears came the sound of numberless birds chirping in the hot morning air.

She yawned comfortably, squirmed, and glanced idly about her. Then she ducked her arms under the bedclothes in horror and hugged the coverlet up to her chin. She had only just become aware of Fleeting Cloud standing motionless at the bedside, a rough tray in his hands.

'For heaven's sake,' she whispered, staring up at him, 'haven't I told you not to creep about like that? It isn't even decent!'

His inscrutable eyes watched her for

a moment, then he set the tray down on the bed edge and silently withdrew. There was coffee — to her profound disgust — but there was also an enormous rasher of ham and two perfectly fried eggs, together with mountains of toast and a great cob of fresh butter. Starved as she had been of such food at home it was a glorious vision.

And there was something else — a folded note next to the coffee pot. She took it up, smoothed out the crease, and read:

Dear Syl,
Ma doesn't usually approve of breakfast in bed: she thinks it's a sign of getting soft! However, I've managed to persuade her to let you have it just this once at least until you have recovered from your travelling. Just get up when you're ready. You'll find us outside somewhere, busy as usual. Please don't think too badly of that story I

spun you. Honest, it was because I'm in love with you.
Neil.

Sylvia read the note through twice, reflected, then laid it on one side and started on the breakfast. By the time she had finished it together with two full cups of coffee, she realized that she had enjoyed it. Usually coffee had a tendency to give her burning pains in the chest. The air? The change in surroundings? The quality of the coffee? She had no idea; she only knew that when she started dressing she felt fitter physically than she could ever remember — but not so fit that she did not indulge in her usual after-breakfast cigarette.

She dressed with great care, her chosen ensemble including jodhpurs, shiny high-heeled half-boots, a blue shirt-blouse of pure silk, and a vermilion kerchief tied loosely at her throat. In fact too loosely: it kept slipping no matter how many times she tied it.

40

Lastly, from her box of jewellery, she took a gold brooch with two diamonds clawed thereon — but she debated before using it. Neil had given it to her in New Orleans to set the seal on their meeting. If she wore it now she would more or less be stating wordlessly that he was back in favour.

'The knot keeps slipping, anyway,' she told her reflection in the mirror, and fixed the brooch in position.

Her finishing touch was a scarlet ribbon through her blonde hair; then she went through into the hall. The first person she saw was Fleeting Cloud, gliding along to the kitchen regions in his noiseless moccasins.

'Where is Ma?' Sylvia asked him boldly, deciding it was about time she revealed some authority.

The redskin motioned to the open ranch-house door. Beyond it the sunlight was flooding down on the porch. Stepping outside, Sylvia came upon Ma Grantham in the act of waddling down the porch steps towards a waiting wagon and team, similar to but more dilapidated than the one in which Sylvia had travelled from the station the previous evening.

'Well, for land's sakes!' Ma stood looking at Sylvia so long and hard that the young woman could feel herself colouring slowly with embarrassment.

'Anything the matter?' she asked sharply.

'Heck, gal, no! I was just a-thinkin' that you're a durned sight purtier than I ever figured. With your hair loose like that instead of with them roll-things in it you're the sassiest bit of young female I ever did see around here . . . Paint spoils it, though. Must you use it, gal?'

'Yes,' Sylvia stated flatly.

Ma shrugged, then turned away suddenly, cupping her hands.

'Hey there, Neil!' she yelled. 'Quit brandin' that yearling an' come an' take a look at the gal you're aimin' to git yourself hitched to.'

Feeling uncomfortable, Sylvia moved as languidly as she could to the porch rail and leaned against it, considering the glory of the morning view. Then Neil's tall, rangy form came in sight, sombrero on the back of his head, his sleeves rolled up on his powerful forearms.

He came to the porch and stood considering the girl in evident admiration. Nor did he fail to notice that she was wearing his brooch. His bronzed features broke into a smile.

'You sure look a picture! Does this mean you're not walking out on me after all?'

'I — er — haven't quite decided yet. I'm prepared to admit that I was jaded last night and maybe hasty in some of my decisions. The air here seems to do me good, too. I can actually drink coffee without getting indigestion. However, if I do decide to stay for a while I insist on paying my share.'

'Not durned likely!' Neil declared, and Ma nodded vigorously.

'If you won't accept payment, is there anything I can do to help around here?

You told me last night, Ma, that I'm strong enough to work like any other girl. Naturally, I'll be going eventually, but until then I may as well make myself useful.'

'Well,' Neil said, 'there's some pens and sties to clean out, but in that natty outfit of yours I don't sort of — '

'She's not a'goin' to clean anythin' out right now,' Ma decided flatly. 'Mebbe later, when she can put on some old clothes.' She looked at the girl. 'We works in this spread ourselves, with Fleet's help. Not a classy ranch where y'can have a foreman an' boys to look after things, so we'd be glad of your help later. First, gal, you want to find out what sort of a place you're in — see the surroundings. I'm aridin' into Nathan's Cleft this mornin' to git some provisions. Mebbe you'd like to string along?'

'I sure would!' Sylvia smiled ruefully. 'That is — I mean — I'd love to.'

'OK then, gal. Hop up on yonder drivin'-seat.'

3

Fateful Meeting

Sylvia mounted quickly on to the wagon and settled alongside Ma Grantham. She gave a start as she beheld a double-barrelled rifle propped handily near Ma's elbow.

'That loaded, Ma?'

'Sure is — an' I can fire as straight an' fast as any man.'

The whip cracked and with the reins in one horny hand Ma set the wagon moving out of the yard. Sylvia's eyes strayed back to the rifle and she frowned.

'But why do you carry it?'

Ma drove on in silence for a time before replying. Then at last the tough old woman seemed to make up her mind.

'Out here there's always danger

45

— an' sometimes a gun's the only law. I'll see that Neil fixes one up for you later. You might run into mad dogs, sufferin' from the heat, snakes, crazy steers, outlaws — an' none of 'em asks questions afore they attack. When that happens you shoot first. Savvy?'

'Did you say — outlaws?'

'The West's full of 'em, gal.' Ma gave a grim chuckle. 'Desperate men that the law'd like to get. With other killings on their consciences why should they worry about more? They're as common in this region as crooks in the big cities, believe you me. Take my advice — never go around without your hardware or you may end up dead.'

'I . . . see.' Sylvia clung on to the seat's narrow rail and in silence considered this disturbing matter. She had just begun to think that she really liked this magnificent natural beauty. Now this new menace had presented itself.

Trying to rid herself of unpleasant thoughts Sylvia came to considering the magnificent countryside once more. Now and again from the mesquite thickets hard by the trail Sonora pigeons swept up, their mating calls echoing shrilly. Unexpectedly there was a glimpse of partridges nestling near the mescal plants. Over the fields of brittle-bush myriads of vermilion fly-catchers flew and shimmered in incredible gyrations. It seemed strange to Sylvia that such beauty could march side by side with shotguns, revolvers, and outlaws.

'Y'see that place up there?' Ma asked presently. Following the old woman's gaze, Sylvia found herself looking at a shack in the remote distances, perched high on a rimrock of the foothills and apparently poised over a deep gorge.

'Yes,' Sylvia nodded. 'Looks like a woodsman's hut.'

'It ain't that. Used to belong to 'Loco' Lannigan. He had a mighty powerful hatred of womenfolk an' went an' shut himself away up there. Crossed in love, I guess,' Ma mused, squinting into the sunshine. 'Anybody who went near him got the pants shot off'n them. Time was when he went on the prowl, too, an' it were mighty tough on any woman he came across. He finished himself by jumpin' into the gorge. I guess that cabin of his must be loaded with ammo if anybody was minded to search for it. He never seemed to run out of bullets, didn't that jigger.'

'Extraordinary personality,' Sylvia commented, with a little shiver.

'Uh-huh. Plenty more of 'em too — mostly harmless. I'll tell you as we go which ones is safe.'

'Much obliged, Ma.'

Sylvia became silent again, trying to settle in her own mind whether she would be sensible to stay in this crazy territory. Yet if she returned home she would have a battle of another sort, with her father.

'That's Nathan's Cleft.' Ma's harsh voice interrupted Sylvia's thoughts. 'Ain't nothin' to look at — but none of these hick towns is. Got guts in it, though — yes, sir! That town were built on beer an' bullets, an' none the worse for it, I reckon.'

Sylvia surveyed it as the wagon swung round the bend in the trail. Nathan's Cleft differed but little from Arrowhead Bend, though it was perhaps a trifle more sprawling. There was the inevitable main street, the boardwalks lining it — then came the usual order of general stores, livery stables, hotel, rooming-houses, sheriff's office, an assayer's, the offices of the *Nathan's Cleft Gazette*, a saloon with a board proclaiming LUCKY CHANCE hanging outside it, and finally a tin tabernacle with a slightly lopsided wooden spire. Outside the general stores Ma drew the buckboard to a halt in clouds of dust, sending a couple of grinning cowpunchers scuttling for safety.

'Howdy, Ma!' one of them yelled, waving his hat. 'Nice piece of goods ridin' with you this mornin'.'

Ma glared at him. 'You button your

lip, Joe Armstrong, afore you gits a crack on your ornery skull!'

'OK, OK, don't git sore!'

Still grinning the men went on their way. Sylvia disdainfully considered the men and women on the boardwalks or moving about the street. They regarded her with frank curiosity as they went by, and some of the men whistled. But they did not dare make any further advances with the formidable Ma Grantham eyeing them.

'Lookee here, gal,' she said dragging a huge wicker basket from the rear of the buckboard, 'you just keep sat here whilst I go in the stores. An' remember — don't start a-mixin' with any of these jiggers: they ain't to be trusted. If any of 'em gits fresh you've always got the rifle.'

Sylvia looked at the weapon nervously.

'But I don't know how to use it!'

'You can if your life depends on it. I got meself tied up with a mountain lion once when I was near your age. Hadn't handled a rod up to then — but I ups it to me shoulder an' shot the critter, clean between the eyes.'

'I don't expect to find mountain lions here, though,' Sylvia pointed out. 'I hope . . . ' she added, glancing about her.

'You may find somethin' worse — men!' Ma's lips tightened. 'Just put the stock agin your shoulder, sight down the barrels — an' only fire if you have to. A murder rap's tough around these parts, but self-defence is different. I guess the gun alone'll be enough to scare any randy guys who come around. Lookin' as purty as you do most anythin' can happen . . . Remember what I told you.'

Ma climbed down into the dust, her elastic-sided boots creaking, and vanished inside the general store.

Sylvia was not exactly frightened — she had too much spirit for that — but she did feel a stranger. Presently she reached out to the rifle and fingered it gently. Gaining a little more courage she lifted it up and laid it across her knees, studying the polished barrels.

'A girl as purty as you don't need a chunk of hardware like that!'

She gave a start and found a puncher regarding her from the side of the buckboard. He was obviously a saddle tramp. His clothes were dirty, his hat smothered in dust, and stubble hid his jaw. He chewed lazily at what Sylvia guessed was a quid of tobacco.

'I don't know you,' she told him coldly, 'and judging from your appearance I don't particularly want to, either.'

'Mebbe I think different,' he replied, then with a sudden grab he seized the rifle butt and yanked the weapon from Sylvia's knees, flinging it into the dust.

'You're a stranger around here, kid,' he decided. 'An' as good-lookin' a one as I ever saw. Case y'don't know it, women around here — specially your sort — have only one use. If you'll come down here I'll explain better what I mean.'

Sylvia slid her way to the other end of the wooden seat. The puncher grinned and lazily watched the movement of her rounded thighs in the close-fitting riding-pants. 'Now is that a way to treat a guy who wants to be pleasant? We set the seal on friendship around here with a kiss, see? Like this . . . '

Suddenly his hands lashed out and seized her ankles. She gave a frantic yell, half of fright and half of pain, as she was yanked from the seat and crashed on her back on the wooden footboard. As she lay struggling the puncher's hands seized her arms and dragged her backwards.

Before she knew what was happening she had been planted down beside him, his powerful arms crushing about her waist and into the small of her back.

'Ain't nothing to get sore about,' he grinned, pinning her hard against him. 'You'll learn that high an' mighty gals don't get far around here. We reckon to soften them up, see, no matter how hard-to-get they play.'

'You dirty great beast!' Sylvia screamed, crimsoning in sudden fury — and her long, well-manicured nails slashed out and dug with fiendish force into his stubbly cheeks.

He only winced for a moment and then stooped to kiss her full on the mouth — but he never got that far. Suddenly Sylvia found herself released as the puncher's grip was torn from her.

A stranger had arrived soundlessly — a big fellow in a black suit and a somewhat clerical-looking hat. Without a word he swung the puncher round to face him, then his right fist came up in a savage uppercut.

The puncher took the blow clean in the mouth and reeled backwards to hit the wheel of the buckboard. Not content with this the stranger pounced on him again, seized his neck, and then began to hammer the puncher's head with relentless violence against the wagon wheel. Not until he gasped for mercy did the onslaught cease. The stranger motioned briefly with the Colt revolver in his right hand.

'Get going, Clinton,' he ordered. 'And keep going! If I ever catch you mauling a woman again I'll tear the stinking hide off you. You've done it a darned sight too often around here. Go on — get!'

Clinton gazed venomously for a moment, wiping a trickle of blood from his mouth with the back of his hand — then he slunk away. The big fellow stood watching him out of sight. When at length he turned he smiled and removed his big, wide-brimmed hat.

'Are you hurt, miss?' he asked concernedly.

'No, I'm not — thanks to you.' Sylvia found her voice unexpectedly hurried.

The lecherous attack, and now the presence of this big, handsome stranger had upset her balance. He was well over six feet, his height levelled by massive bulk. She guessed him at perhaps thirty years of age. His face was deeply tanned, with sharp brown eyes and a wealth of gleaming, sloe-black hair. She noticed his teeth were unusually large in front and spotlessly white.

'You're a stranger around here, I think?' he said. 'In fact you must be: I'd remember if I'd seen you before.'

'Yes, I am a stranger here.' Sylvia got her voice and emotions in hand again. 'I'm staying with the Granthams at the Blue Circle.'

The big fellow smiled broadly. 'Ma Grantham's quite a character, isn't she?'

'I suppose she is. But I'm pretty sure her heart's in the right place.'

'Yes, even if the rest of her's cast-iron.' The tall stranger gave a wry smile and then continued, 'I'm Carl Naylor. I own the Lucky Chance saloon down the street here, and my ranch is about five miles away at Cragpoint. The Leaning L is my spread. If ever in your travels you get around that far you'll be mighty welcome to drop in.'

He held out his big hand and it swallowed Sylvia's dainty fingers. He looked at her with his intense dark eyes for a moment, then releasing his grip he picked up the rifle from the dust and gave it back to her.

'Nice hardware,' he commented.

Sylvia took it gingerly. 'I suppose it is, but I don't like the idea of ever using it.'

'All the same, when you get a *hombre* like Clinton fooling about, it's justifiable to plug him tight with lead. Surprises me someone hasn't done it before now.'

'You mean, Mr Naylor, that had I shot him nobody would have said anything?'

'That's right,' he smiled. 'Self-defence is quite a strong line with the law around these parts — 'specially with attractive women. You'd do well to remember that, Miss — er . . . ?'

'Sylvia Carfax.'

'I like it,' he said approvingly. 'Got as much class about its ring as you have about your figure.'

Sylvia laughed, trying to decide whether or not she really liked Carl

Naylor. She had not resolved the issue when an emphatic voice exclaimed:

'Lookee here, gal, I thought I told you to take care who you spoke to around here? Now git back on that wagon and stay there!'

Sylvia was so astonished she just stared as Ma Grantham came lumbering heavily round the rear of the buckboard after having heaved the provisions into it. Putting her hands on her hips she squinted up at Carl Naylor in the sunlight.

'I might have known that if I turned me back five minutes you'd be around, Carl! Leave the gal alone an' git back to your den of thieves. If it's women you're after, an' I s'pose it is, there's plenty you can find without monkeyin' around here.'

'Durn it, Ma, anyone would think you don't like me.' Naylor chuckled.

'I don't!' Ma snapped. 'Never have done! Too slick with the gals — but this is one gal you'll keep your mitts away from or answer straight to me — Go

on, gal, up on that seat like I told you,'
she added impatiently.

'When I'm ready,' Sylvia responded.
'You shouldn't be slighting Mr Naylor
— he has a good reason for being here.
He saved me from a most odious
experience.'

'He did, huh?' Ma growled suspiciously. 'Like as not he only did it for
some gain to himself — either now or
later.'

Indignant, Sylvia related the incident
with Clinton in detail. Ma listened, but
was unimpressed.

'Don't make no difference.' She
motioned again to the buckboard. 'Git
up on that seat, gal.'

'I'm afraid the old warhorse means
it,' Naylor said, sighing. 'If you'll allow
me, Miss Carfax . . . '

His big hands clamped suddenly at
either side of her slender waist and she
was lifted effortlessly upwards and
deposited on the footboard. She sat
down slowly, amazed at his strength. He
grinned up at her and replaced his hat

on his dark head, then he looked grimly at Ma Grantham.

'Sooner you stop slanging me in public, Ma, the better I'll like it,' he said curtly.

'I speak as I find, Carl Naylor!' Ma spat emphatically into the dust. 'Lay off this gal or it'll be too bad for you, big as y'are. Now git out of my way!'

She tried to push him aside roughly, but only succeeded in being helped on to the wagon herself. She glared at him over her shoulder.

'If I'm ever weak enough to need your help, Carl, I'll feed meself to the coyotes!' she told him. 'Git away from me. I don't want to start washin' before I git back to the spread.'

Sinking heavily into the driving-seat, she flicked the whip across the horses. She did not look back at Naylor — but Sylvia did, waving to him as he stood with hat upraised once more — Then, suddenly, Sylvia found her arm snatched down to her side.

'It's time you started gettin' some

sense, gal,' Ma declared fiercely as she hurtled the buckboard and team out of the main street. 'I'm not a-blamin' you for talkin' to Carl Naylor because he's the type as gits all the gals around him. But he's the wrong sort for you.'

'What's the matter with him? At least he behaved like a gentleman in saving me from that low-down tramp.'

'Listen, gal, Carl Naylor never did anythin' for anybody, 'specially a gal as attractive as you, without havin' a good reason for it. He did it to get himself introduced to you, that's all. He's up to every dodge on the board when he sees a gal he takes a fancy to.'

'Preposterous! He could have introduced himself anyway. He isn't exactly the bashful type.'

Ma watched the dusty trail for a moment or two, thinking; then she came back to the attack. 'I've lived around here for years an' I know the ones y'can trust and the ones y'can't. Naylor's made more gals unhappy than I can remember — and he takes durned good care he never marries any of 'em. Love 'em and leave 'em — that's his line. He gits away with it because he's wealthy an' influential an' — '

'Wealthy and influential?' Sylvia interrupted, starting. 'You mean like Neil said *he* was until I discovered otherwise?'

Ma aimed a grim look. 'You needn't start rakin' that up again. I thought I made it plain enough last night just how things stand with us?'

'I'm not raking it up; I'm just thinking that Mr Naylor seems to be all the things Neil *should* have been. Now I am out here, Ma, with my bridges more or less burned behind me, I'm out for the best opportunity, and don't you forget it! I know you married a cowhand and were happy ever after — but perhaps you and I aren't built in quite the same way.'

'Well, for land's sakes!' Ma stared at the girl in wonder. 'Are you tryin' to tell me that, livin' under my roof with Neil alongside, you're thinkin' of standin' him up an' goin' after Carl Naylor?'

'And if I was?' Sylvia contemplated the sunny pasturelands.

'Do that an' you'll have no part of my homestead!' Ma snapped. 'You can stay, an' welcome, just as long as you marry Neil an' settle down — once you've gotten used to things. But I won't stand for you runnin' about after anybody else, 'specially not Carl Naylor! He's a dead wrong 'un — I'm warnin' you!'

Sylvia dropped the argument. She wanted to think about it. Ma interpreted the silence as meaning that the notion of pursuing Naylor had died on its feet, and consequently she was quite genial again by the time the Blue Circle had once more been reached.

Neil came strolling from one of the outhouses as the buckboard drew up.

'Everything all right?' he enquired, helping Sylvia down.

'Would ha' been but for the gal here meetin' up with that no-good Naylor,' Ma answered, heaving the provisions on to the porch.

Neil's expression changed. Sylvia noticed a hardening of his powerful mouth. 'What about Carl?' he demanded. 'Did he try something on you, Syl? If he did I'm riding straight into town to blast the living day — '

'He saved me from a tramp,' Sylvia interposed. 'And that was the act of a gentleman even if your Ma does seem to think otherwise.'

'That's just what you were meant to think,' Neil retorted. 'He got that polish of his from a pretty good education back in Carson City — but he's ornery and no-account just the same. Keep away from him, Syl. He's not your type.'

'And you are?' One delicately lined eyebrow rose.

'At least I take care to live clean — and that's more than Carl Naylor does.'

Dead silence. Then Ma spoke.

'I was a-tellin' the gal here that it ain't safe for her to play around in this territory without hardware. Fix her up with a gun, Neil — an' show her how to fire the blamed thing. Seems she don't know a barrel from a butt.'

'You're right,' Sylvia admitted. 'But I still don't think I need a gun.'

'You have to protect yourself,' Neil told her. 'Wait here while I fix you up.' He went striding into the ranch house and returned after a while with a small revolver in his hand. He held it out in his extended palm and Sylvia looked at it.

'It's a thirty-two,' he explained. 'Not the man-sized rod usually packed around here, but just about right for you. Try it for size.'

Sylvia did so awkwardly, then swiftly handed it back. 'It seems all right, Neil, but honestly I'd rather not bother.'

'If you're going to stay on in this region you must learn how to shoot,' Neil insisted. 'If you're not staying on . . . ' He shrugged, 'Well, if you're not I guess there wouldn't be much point in my wasting time showing you how to use it. Plenty else I have to do around here.'

'I'm staying,' Sylvia said quietly. 'At least for a while, if only for my health. I suppose, for my own sake, you'd better show me . . . '

So her training began, and by the time Fleeting Cloud had rung the triangle outside the ranch door to announce that lunch was ready Sylvia had at least lost her fear of the gun, even though her shooting was not particularly accurate.

She spent part of the scorching afternoon in further practice; then she gave up for a while and went into the ranch-house to change. While in the midst of cleaning out one of the cowsheds, Neil was astonished to behold Sylvia approaching in heavy boots and overlarge Levis, her sleeves rolled up well beyond her dimpled elbows.

'Ma loaned me these,' she explained. 'Seemed to me it is about time I did a bit of work; gun practice can wait. What am I supposed to do?' She broke off and looked about her, her nostrils offended by the deadening stench of the place.

Neil considered, realizing her inexperience.

'If you can get the cows in from pasture I'll do the milking. Ma's busy doin' some steer-branding.'

Sylvia blundered out into the yard again in her big boots. She headed determinedly for the pasture where the cows were grazing. All of them were obviously ready for milking.

Gingerly she opened the big gate that led into the yard, then swung her arm in a come-hither motion.

'Mooo!' she called. 'Nice cow! Come on . . . '

One or two of the beasts raised their heads, chewed impassively and fixed their goggling eyes upon her. Her knees quivered a little but she held her ground.

'What in blue tarnation are you doin', gal?' Ma Grantham suddenly appeared, gave Sylvia one look of profound contempt and then went on into the pasture.

'Hey, you!' she yelled, with a voice worthy of a champion hog-caller. 'Git to hell over here!'

Every cow moved as though drawn by irresistible power. Fascinated, Sylvia watched them come filing in, Ma standing with hands on hips, eyeing them.

'Doesn't seem as though I'm much good with cattle, does it?' Sylvia sighed.

'You're durned tootin',' Ma told her candidly. 'There's plenty of other jobs, though — gettin' the fowl houses cleaned up, loadin' that manure into the yard, fixin' the hayloft for when we start garnerin' — An' garnerin'll mebbe sweat some of that durned paint out of your system. Best go an' see what else Neil wants done,' Ma said, and returned her attention to the cows.

Sylvia turned and went in search of Neil again. She found him loading evil-smelling manure that reminded her of buckets of the most pungent cabbage water she had ever smelled.

'I'm no good with cows,' she said plaintively. 'What else have you?'

'Grab a fork and do as I do,' he said briefly. She did as bidden and began to help him, working until her back muscles began to crack.

Only then did she give in and return to the less arduous — even if more exacting — task of learning how to shoot. She kept at it until early evening, loathing the smell of herself with her overalls caked in dung; then by this time her fingers were aching intolerably and she could do no more.

Neil, who had been watching her from beside a tree as she tried to plug a tin at fifty feet, came forward with a grin as he saw her passable efficiency.

'Now I feel better,' he announced, 'because I'll know that when you're out on your own — which won't be often if I can help it — you'll at least have some protection from *hombres* like Clinton.'

'I'm glad *you're* feeling better. I never felt so fed up and overridden with horrible smells in all my life!' The girl contemplated the .32 in her hand. 'And this isn't exactly going to be a pleasure to carry around, either. What do you suggest I do — I don't fancy wearing a gunbelt and holster!'

Neil considered. 'Your best bet is to wear a shoulder holster, then you can keep it out of sight inside your blouse, or shirt. That way you'll keep the element of surprise.'

'Uh-huh, I can do that,' Sylvia agreed pensively. 'But what do I do in the case of an evening gown with short sleeves? Do you think it would show?'

'Be a bulge, mebbe . . . ' Neil frowned. 'I can't see you ever needing to wear an evening gown, though — '

'I'm wearing one tonight. I intend,' Sylvia explained, 'to get on better terms with Carl Naylor, and apologize to him for Ma's atrocious behaviour this morning.'

'But you can't do that,' Neil exclaimed, seizing her shoulders. 'He's a wrong 'un! You don't suppose we'd say that if it weren't true, do you?'

'I'll find that out for myself — and I don't believe it, anyway. After this afternoon's experiences I feel the odd girl out! I don't understand ranch life, and from the smell of it I'm not sure I want to. I just can't limit myself to everyday jobs.'

'Anyway, you're not going with Carl Naylor!' Neil snapped. 'Somebody else mebbe, but as it is — '

'I think otherwise. I've learned all this shooting with that in mind, because in going into his saloon to find him I know I'll meet plenty of tough characters. Now I feel I can look after myself.'

The girl shook away Neil's hand from her shoulder, and went into the ranch house. On the way to her room she found the small holster to which the .32 belonged hanging behind the door. Equipped with it she continued on her way — and did not reappear until the evening meal.

Ma and Neil watched her silently as, resplendent in a black gown with sequins glinting in the lamplight, she took her place at the table. Her hair was magnificently arranged in puffs and rolls, drawn up from her ears and forehead. The short sleeves of the gown came half-way to her rounded elbows.

There was a long, uncomfortable silence. Fleeting Cloud came in with the meal and set it down. He went out again with wraithlike quietness.

'It's stew,' Ma said at last, raising the lid of the dish. 'Too ornery for a gal like you, I s'pose?'

'On the contrary, Ma, I'm looking forward to trying it. I seem to have lost my indigestion.'

Throughout the meal there was only desultory conversation, then, as Sylvia excused herself and made to rise from the table, Ma snapped:

'So you're still aimin' to go huntin' for Carl Naylor, are you? Guess you're just too plain dumb obstinate to listen to reason!'

'I'm not obstinate, Ma; just interested in people. And I'm not anxious to see Mr Naylor again because I'm in love with him, or anything stupid like that. I simply think he's in my class as a friend. I just *can't* assimilate all this rustic atmosphere at once. If I don't get some kind of diversion akin to city life I'll go crazy.'

'Oh, let her try it, Ma,' Neil interrupted, before his mother could continue her protests. 'Let her learn the hard way.'

Ma mused on this, then gave a brief nod. 'OK, son. Reckon you're right.'

Sylvia sensed some deeper meaning in the exchange, but what it was she simply did not care. The thought of spending what was left of the evening in this ranch house, listening to gossip about cattle or vegetables, was intolerable. When she reached the door of the room Neil called after her.

'Nathan's Cleft is a good five miles from here, Syl. How do you figure on getting there?'

'Use the wagon and team, of course. I watched Ma driving it this morning, so there's no reason why I can't do the same, is there?'

'That wagon and them cayuses stay where they is tonight, gal,' Ma declared, her mouth setting. 'They need to be rested. No single hoss of mine is leavin' here either — not as you could git your legs astride one in that blamed dress, anyways.'

Sylvia tightened her mouth. 'So that's your attitude is it? All right, I'll walk! Hanged if I won't!'

'Exercise'll do you good,' Ma commented shortly. 'Good riddance to you!'

Sylvia swept from the room, banging the door. She collected her light dustcoat from her room and presently set off into the cool, starlit night, without a backward glance.

Gaining the trail that led to Nathan's Cleft she walked along it resolutely, but none too elegantly. Now and again in her advance she stopped and listened, but except for the occasional distant wailing of a coyote under the stars, or the remote sounds of a mountain lion, there was nothing immediately frightening to her. But there were lots of smaller worries that brought her hand clutching towards her shoulder where the .32 lay buried in readiness. Packrats had a habit of scuttling suddenly over her feet, seizing her in a cold chill; or there would be a rustling nearby as perhaps a ground squirrel went on his way. For the rest there was only the intangible enigma of the Western night — the brilliant stars, the rising moonlight to the east, and the mighty barrier of the mountains looming blacker than night itself.

The wind, bringing with it the smell of juniper, oak and cedar, blew softly across her heated cheeks as she stumbled onwards. At the end of what she judged was two miles of the journey her determination was beginning to weaken. She was feeling tired and pains were commencing to shoot up her legs from walking on the iron-hard ground. She sat by the trail presently, contemplating the glittering diadem of the sky and wondering if she ought to admit herself beaten and return to the ranch.

But she was a Carfax at heart, obstinate and tough beneath her frills and fineries. She would not give the Granthams the satisfaction of seeing her trailing back, as they no doubt expected she would. Of one thing she felt reasonably sure — Carl Naylor would never permit her to walk home.

The moon had fully risen when Sylvia came at last within view of the lights of Nathan's Cleft. Her feet were leaden and her calves aching as she gained the main street, making her way slowly up it and trying to appear as though she had just alighted from some conveyance or other.

Realizing her light dustcoat and uncovered blonde head were attracting unwelcome attention she made for the boardwalk and strolled with dignity along it, the kerosene-lamps hanging from the buildings illuminating her way.

Though none of the idling punchers she passed made any attempt to molest her she could feel their eyes watching her — and once she heard significant whistles.

Ignoring such distractions she came at length to the Lucky Chance and peered over the top of the batwing doors. Here was the toughest of all tasks — until she had gained the protection of Carl Naylor, anyway.

Plucking up courage, she swung the batwing doors open and stepped beyond them. Halting, she looked about her, her hands deep in the pockets of her dustcoat.

4

True Colours

The room was long and lofty, lighted by four oil-lamps hanging on a beam at equal intervals. In the tobacco-fumed distances upon a palm-bedecked rostrum, a two-man orchestra — violin and piano — was striving to make a noise above the general din, whilst in the opposite direction there stood the bar, lined with cowpunchers, some with one foot on the brass rail two inches from the floor level, others just lounging and staring at Sylvia in blank amazement.

The barkeep caught sight of her in the ornate mirrors at the back of the bar and spun round. Never had he seen any girl so modern and so good-looking walk into this stinking den of cowpunchers, gamblers, storekeepers, half-breeds, and saddle tramps. The women were staring as well, most of them overpainted and underdressed, conversing over well-filled glasses or else sullenly sitting alone waiting until they attracted attention.

Sylvia's gaze lifted beyond the immediate focus of the occupied tables and contemplated instead the faro and roulette section crowded with riotous players. In another direction, tense poker-games were in progress. She wondered how anybody who had smelled the pure freshness of the night air could possibly turn in here and waste an evening. Lacking the necessary nerve as yet to step forward, her eyes searched anxiously for Carl Naylor as she remained by the batwings.

Evidently Naylor had seen her, however, for unexpectedly she found him at her elbow, his great form looming above her, the polished black of his hair gleaming in the oil-light. The soft shirt he had been wearing had now been replaced by a big stiff shield of white front, a shoestring tie dangling down it.

'Miss Carfax isn't it?' he asked. 'About the last place I expected to meet you again.'

'I was just — er — passing through,' Sylvia explained, glad of his protection. 'I thought I had perhaps better look to apologize for Ma Grantham's behaviour this morning. I felt responsible . . . '

'Mighty nice of you, Miss Carfax — but nobody takes much notice of what Ma says. She treats most men and women as though they'd just crawled out of a crack. Folks around here have gotten used to her.'

'Just the same, Mr Naylor, I think she insulted you. I still don't think she really believes you saved me from being assaulted by that man — '

'Between you and me, Miss Carfax, I don't care whether she believes it or not. All I'm interested in is that you took the trouble to come. I'd intended looking you up at the Blue Circle myself . . . ' Naylor's gaze dropped from Sylvia's grey-blue eyes to her feet.

He gave another grin. 'Looks like you picked up plenty of dust,' he commented. 'And I guess you sure didn't ride a horse in that finery! Sure you were just passing through?'

'I . . . ' Sylvia stopped, embarrassed, and Carl patted her arm.

'I'll lay evens that Ma Grantham and Neil didn't like the idea of your coming here — so you've had to walk it!'

'That's right,' Sylvia admitted quietly.

'I thought as much. In that case, you need a drink,' Carl decided. 'And you shall have it in peace, too, not amongst this bunch of tramps in here. Just come along with me.'

Sylvia found herself directed through the midst of the tables and passing within inches of the watching men and women. Nobody spoke, and no man dared to make a pass at her with Carl beside her. Finally they left the smoky poolroom behind and entered a quiet little semi-office at the rear. Carl lighted the solitary oil-lamp and it glowed on to a small table, casting faint illumination on furniture in the shadows.

'My private room,' he explained. 'Reserved for special customers, or when I've deals to discuss with cattlemen and such. Let me have your coat, then you can sit back and relax.'

Sylvia nodded and drew her arms out of her coat, settling afterwards at the table and taking the cigarette Carl offered from a gold case. He struck a match for her, his dark eyes looking into hers over the dancing flame.

'I don't think I told you this morning that you're mighty pretty, Miss Carfax,' he said, waving the match into extinction. 'But if I did, then it goes double . . . Now, what'll you have to drink?'

'Brandy and soda, thanks.'

The saloon owner's eyebrows rose. 'No soft drinks? Guess you like to drink hard, huh?'

'Not exactly hard, but I don't like wishy-washy stuff.'

Carl nodded, grinned, and turned to the door, shouting his order across the crowded room beyond. A waiter brought the drinks in presently, then retired and closed the door. Unnoticed by Sylvia, Carl turned the key and slipped it in his vest pocket. Then he came to the table and settled down. He poured out the drinks and he and Sylvia had both drained their glasses before he spoke again.

'I'm flattered to think that you'd walk all the way from the Blue Circle spread just to apologize for Ma Grantham. Or was that the real reason?' he inquired drily.

Sylvia was feeling unusually amiable now with the brandy warming her.

'Matter of fact no, Mr Naylor — '

'All my friends call me Carl. Aren't you one of them?'

'I hope so. And you can call me Sylvia — or Syl, if you prefer.'

'Syl it is, then. Not quite so starchy. Out in this part of the world we're all good friends. But go on — you were saying why you came here.'

'I came,' Sylvia said, considering her empty glass, 'because I'd like you as a friend. I'm used to mixing in a circle where there is money, high life, plenty of movement. Once you get into that sort of groove you don't easily get out of it.'

'No, I guess not. Sounds to me then that you won't like the Blue Circle much!'

'I like it all right but it isn't frightfully exciting. Ma Grantham told me that you're influential, wealthy, and amount to something around here . . . ' Sylvia stopped for a moment and then said directly, 'In other words you are what Neil Grantham was *supposed* to be. He let me down frightfully, you know.'

'He did? How?'

Sylvia explained and then wondered why she had been so liberal with her information. That large brandy-and-soda she had consumed had not tasted as it usually did. Now it was confusing her thoughts and tongue to an amazing extent. Usually she was seasoned enough to stand not one but several brandy-and-sodas.

'In that case,' Carl said easily, sitting back in his chair and still watching her, 'I guess you need the kind of company I can give you. There's no doubt about my authority around here, Syl. Be real nice to me, and I can very soon give you the kind of life you like having — and you can forget all about that impoverished puncher Neil Grantham! He's just too blamed honest! A bit of good business on the side never did any guy any harm, but he just don't seem able to see things that way. I never could stand a critter who walks around with an invisible prayer book in his fist.'

Sylvia squeezed finger and thumb into her eyes as she saw two Carl Naylors for a moment. At the same time she could hear the dull beating of her heart in her ears. Carl watched her intently, then got up and caught at her shoulders.

'Something wrong?' he asked, affecting surprise.

'I — I don't quite know what's

wrong, Carl! Either that was very powerful brandy or else this room is too warm. I feel — horribly faint.'

Carl straightened up, then as he withdrew his hand over her right shoulder he paused as his hand touched the hard outline of the shoulder holster. Against the black of her dress it was hardly visible.

'What's this?' he asked coldly. 'Not very complimentary, is it? Makes it look as if you don't trust me.'

'I have — to protect myself.' Sylvia felt as if she were rocking. She giggled foolishly. 'Can't just walk about wi' a gun on my hip. Take away th' shurprise — Neil told me. Anyway, you're wearing one!' She squinted at the walnut-butted, pearl-inlaid Colt swinging at Carl's hip. He put a big hand over it.

'I have to. I run a saloon full of tough characters. Not like you . . . It isn't ladylike — even less so to carry it concealed. You'd better hand it over, Syl.'

'Supposin' I don't want to?' Sylvia argued sleepily.

'Then I'll take it myself!' Carl was gazing at her fixedly. 'Women and hardware unsettle me — they don't know how to handle it.'

Sylvia did not answer. She sat regarding him stupidly, her mouth open and her eyes misted. He grinned widely.

'I'll take it then,' he said, 'and seal our friendship with a kiss at the same time, huh?'

Life stirred back into Sylvia for a moment. Somewhere in the depths of her dulled, confused brain she realized that Ma Grantham had been right. She made to grab at her hidden gun but her arms were pinned back hard against the chair, her struggling useless as Carl kissed her with fierce vehemence — then twice more.

Gasping, too dizzy and sick to realize what she was doing, she felt his hand tear her costly dress down the front; then the hardness of the gun-holster suddenly went as he pulled it from beneath her armpit. She felt clumsily at where it had been and then looked up to see Carl looming gigantic in the lamplight, studying the weapon. Finally he tossed it contemptuously on the table.

'I — I don't believe that was brandy you gave me,' she whispered, swinging unsteadily on her feet and trying vainly to claw her ripped dress back into position. 'You — you did somethin' to it. The floor's rockin' so much under me I can hardly — hardly stand up!'

Carl strode forward suddenly, lifted her in his arms and carried her to the couch. Then he looked down on her, his dark eyes cold and hard.

'You're the kind of woman I've been needing for a long time,' he said deliberately. 'Looks, figure, youth — you've got everything! You want to be friends, you say? OK, there's one sure way to begin — and don't start blaming me for what may happen. You walked into this of your own accord, just asking for it . . .'

He stooped towards her, then twisted round in surprise. His amazement changed to fury as the glass of the window near the couch suddenly splintered. Fast though his hand blurred down to his Colt it was not fast enough. He found himself looking into the levelled barrel of a .45, merciless eyes behind it.

'No you don't, Carl,' Neil Grantham's voice warned him. 'Stand up straight and get your filthy paws off Syl! And hurry it up, damn you!'

Grim-faced, Carl obeyed, knowing better than to argue. Neil knocked out the rest of the glass with his elbow, then slid through the frame into the room, his revolver still aimed directly at Carl's heart.

'Good job I came along,' he said coldly, taking the saloon owner's gun and throwing it into a far corner. 'Thanks for not drawing the window shade. Gave me a chance to see what was going on. I figured you might try something like this, so I trailed Syl to be sure. She doesn't know you as well as I do.'

Carl remained silent, his hands raised, a glitter in his dark eyes. On the couch Sylvia stirred weakly, holding her head. Finally she twisted round far enough to be able to see Neil towering beside her.

'Neil . . . ' she whispered huskily. 'How — how did you get here?'

'Never mind now,' he answered. 'Just count yourself lucky that I did.' He backed to the door and tried it futilely. Glancing at the empty keyhole, he slowly holstered his gun. 'I guess locking the door is just the way I want it, Carl,' he commented, returning into the centre of the room. 'You did it to stop Syl getting out — but it can also stop anybody getting in.'

'So what?' Carl snapped, his eyes darting to the corner where lay his gun, then moving to the table where he had flung down Sylvia's small .32.

'So I think it's time your manners were polished up a bit,' Neil said. 'It doesn't make no odds to me what you do — or have done — to girls I don't even know. But it matters a heap when you start mauling Syl. She belongs to me!'

'Not from what she told me! And I reckon no girl who's decent would walk into a saloon to find a man she hardly knows if she — '

Carl got no further. Neil's big fist suddenly flashed up with savage violence. Carl jerked his head to one side but not quickly enough. He absorbed the blow on the side of his jaw and it rocked him for a moment — then he dived forward, his hands struggling for Neil's throat.

Neil was ready for him. He delivered a hammer punch into the saloon owner's stomach, doubling him in anguish. Not a second later a left hook slammed up and took Carl under the jaw. Winded and dazed with the impact he reeled backwards into the wall and half slid to the floor . . .

Then he realized he was only an inch

or two from his revolver. He dived for it and Neil flung himself at him. Instantly Carl jack-knifed his legs and shot them out again. Neil got the boot-heels in his stomach and was catapulted backwards into the table. He clutched at it, gasping, saving the lamp from spilling over in a chaos of flame and oil.

'All right, damn you, straighten up!' Carl snarled at him, standing erect with his Colt levelled. 'I'm going to drill you neat, Neil, just the same as I do to any guy who muscles in on my privacy — *God*!' Carl gasped in sudden anguish, doubling up, and the revolver clattered out of his hand.

The interruption had been so swift and soundless it had hardly been noticeable. A thin, flashing line had come from the smashed window straight for Carl's gun hand. Now he dragged out the stained blade of a knife that had transfixed him through the right palm. The knife fell to the floor and he stood clutching his brimming right hand in the fingers of his left, scarlet threads coursing down them.

Neil twirled round and then grinned as he beheld Fleeting Cloud easing himself silently into the room. He picked up his knife, wiped the blade on his pants, then returned it to its sheath. This accomplished he stood looking at the wounded saloon owner with his inscrutable eyes.

'You dirty, no-account redskin!' Carl screamed at him. 'I'll tear you in pieces for this before I'm through. You too, Grantham! There's nobody born who can do these things to me without me getting even!'

'Let's get out of this den of vice,' Neil said.

He picked up Sylvia's coat and tossed it over his shoulder. Her gun he jammed in his belt and then added: 'Keep an eye on this skunk, Fleet, whilst I get Syl outside.'

The Indian nodded, his only protection his knife — but the fact that his sinewy hand lay in readiness on its hilt was enough to deter Carl from attempting anything. In any case his gunhand was too badly hurt for him to try using it, so he stood watching, gripping his sliced palm, as Neil hauled the now unconscious girl into his arms and clambered with her through the window.

Only then did Fleeting Cloud start to retreat — and he escaped through the window without Carl risking anything. Then Carl dashed to the opening as the Indian vanished, but he and Neil had already disappeared with Sylvia into the night . . .

Sylvia began to find her senses returning to her as she felt the steady jogging of the horse and the cool night wind blowing in her face. She stirred to the realization that she was seated sidesaddle, Neil's arm holding her tightly round the waist whilst with his free hand he gripped his sorrel's reins. They were moving along at a steady trot under the stars.

'Learned any better sense yet, Syl?' Neil asked grimly, as her throbbing head lay against his shoulder.

'All right, I admit I was wrong.' The girl sighed. 'At least I found out for myself that Naylor's a no-good, just as you and Ma said.'

'In case you're not aware of it, Syl, you've made things mighty difficult.'

Sylvia sat up as she felt her strength returning.

'It seems to me that it was Carl who made all the going.'

'And I had to beat him up because of it — and Fleet landed a knife through his hand. He'll want revenge for that.'

'I suppose he will,' Sylvia admitted. 'But you can take care of yourself.'

'I guess so. From now on you, me, and Ma and Fleet have got to be ready for just anything. When Carl sets out to get anybody he goes the long, sly way round — but he always manages to swing it. Chiefly because he's got power and money. A dangerous man to have as an enemy.'

Sylvia was silent for a space, watching

Fleeting Cloud as he rode on steadily ahead in the moonlight.

'This . . . horse of yours walks lame,' she said, in an effort to change the subject.

'Yeah — calloused foot. Crooked shoe.' Neil was curt.

Sylvia tried another tack. 'What do you suppose knocked me out? I never went like that before on just one brandy and soda.'

'You're not the first girl Naylor's drugged,' Neil told her. 'After all, it's a simple way to break down resistance, isn't it?'

'So that was it!' Sylvia gave a little shudder. 'That amounts to attempted rape! Great heavens, if I reported this he could get penal servitude for a trick like that — '

'You'd get nowhere! This is a particularly tough part of the old West. The sooner you get that fact through your skull the better. Men like Naylor take what they want and do what they want, simply because they're powerful and can shoot faster than the sheriff or any of his men. Only one law in this region, Syl — gun law, and Naylor's a past master at it. You can be thankful that I decided to follow you and keep a watch on your safety.'

Sylvia remained silent, lost in thought until the journey had been finished. Then as Neil lifted her down gently from the sorrel she said:

'Neil, I'm willing to admit that I've been an idiot. I won't see Carl again — or anybody else whom you or Ma don't consider . . . savoury.'

'Bit late to think of it, isn't it?' he said. 'I guess the damage is done now. We haven't seen the last of Carl Naylor, don't you forget it.'

Sylvia turned away angrily and went striding across the moonlit yard to the ranch house.

★   ★   ★

It was a very chastened Sylvia who, after a disturbed night, settled down at the breakfast table the following morning.

She had returned to her silk blouse and jodhpurs, the gold pin in her vermilion kerchief, and the scarlet ribbon through her cascading blonde hair. But she looked tired and jaded and there were little furrows in her usually smooth forehead.

'Mornin', gal,' Ma Grantham greeted her bluntly, eyeing her in her unnerving fashion. 'You look as though you've bin round the countryside tied to a cayuse's tail.'

'I hardly slept at all,' Sylvia admitted; then as she saw that Ma and Neil were looking at her in some puzzlement she added:

'Yes, I've left off my make-up — and that's made me look pale. I don't feel so bad really. Breakfast should put me right.'

Fleeting Cloud came in silently and set down a rasher of ham and two eggs in front of her. She sniffed appreciatively at the aroma.

'That's one good thing you've left behind anyways,' Ma decided. 'Spring water's good enough for any skin around here . . . You look a hundred per cent better without the paint, gal.'

Sylvia remained quiet, studying the tablecloth idly. The previous night when she had come into the ranch house Ma had not spoken a word. Since her mood was now more tractable, it seemed safe to assume that Neil had managed to talk her round.

'Git this coffee an' some food inside you, gal,' Ma instructed, handing it over. 'You'll feel better — an' I hope you'll have more sense in future than to go against what we knows is good for you.'

'After last night you can be sure I'll take heed,' Sylvia responded, and gave a little shiver. 'I've never been so mistaken in all my life as I was in Carl Naylor.'

'You're not the first gal to be fooled. He's as deceptive as a rattler.' Ma cracked toast noisily between her magnificent teeth. 'But if he comes a-snoopin' around here I'll drill him neat with no questions. Be glad to do the community a service. An' how's about you, gal?' she broke off. 'Time you was gettin' officially engaged to Neil, ain't it?'

'I still want to think about it,' Sylvia answered, looking at her plate. 'I haven't been here so very long, Ma,' she went on, glancing up for a moment. 'I don't even know yet if the district will suit me properly. I wish you'd let me pay my way while I think things over — '

'Forget payment,' Ma snapped. 'You're welcome to stay long as you like, but you must take your part. We work mighty hard just to stay alive.'

'Yes, so I've noticed.'

'Then y'can do somethin' about it. Help us around the spread.'

'I'm quite willing to, only I don't seem to be much of a success at it. And I just can't cope with the smell!'

Ma guffawed loudly. 'What the heck's

a bit of a stink when there's work to be done? If animals make you sick, gal, then be sick, and git it over with. No other way around here. Neil will show you what he wants doin'. I told you the first night you came here you've got a strong body under them fancy curves. It just wants toughening, an' by cracky it'll get it!'

During the morning, and indeed throughout the remainder of that day, Sylvia found that Ma had certainly not exaggerated. Despite her natural repugnance to farm life, and the farm effluvia which wafted constantly about her in the blazing heat, she helped about the ranch and outhouses, was shown how to milk the cows, and clean out the pens and sties.

She finished the day with throbbing muscles, a stiff back, an irremovable smell of manure in her nostrils, and an appetite which astounded her. When Neil and Ma announced that they must return to their normal practice of retiring shortly after sunset — so they could be up at daybreak — she raised no objections concerning herself.

By ten o'clock she was fast asleep, her last thought as her senses fled being one of surprise that she had not touched a cigarette all day.

As the days passed, smoking had become one of the least interesting of her habits. Like her make-up compact, the cigarette case lay forgotten in the dresser drawer in her room. It was a week later when she came across it — a week that had hardened her physique amazingly and given her a zest for living which she had never before thought possible.

She considered the cigarettes as she tipped them from the case into her palm — then she crushed them into dry powder and flung them through the half-open window.

That evening, as she, Neil, and Ma sat on the porch whilst Fleeting Cloud was clearing away the remains of the supper, Neil came round to the subject of Carl Naylor again.

'I can't understand why that jigger's lyin' low,' he mused, rolling himself a cigarette and considering the brilliant light of the setting sun behind the range.

'Probably he knows when he's licked.'

Sylvia, relaxed in the basket-chair, sniffed appreciatively at the aromas of the evening breeze, cooling and delicately perfumed after the murderous heat of the day.

'Not Carl Naylor,' Ma told her, swinging back and forth in a rocking-chair with her gnarled hands locked over her middle. 'An' it seems to me that that means that he might . . . ' She paused and stared hard into the distance.

'Somebody a-comin',' she announced. 'Mebbe we talked of the devil an' this is him now. If so I'll sure give the critter somethin' to remember!'

Neal eased his gun from its holster in readiness, then slipped it back again as he realized it would not be needed. The lone rider was not Naylor but a much older man, bearded, thin-shouldered, mounted on a chestnut mare.

'Looks like Mal Newcomb to me,' Ma said, peering under her hand. 'From the Forty-Nine spread further down the valley. I wonder what he can be a-wantin' with us? I ain't seen him around these regions in some time.'

With Sylvia beside him Neil sat watching the rider as he came up and dismounted as he gained the ranch. Then Newcomb tied the animal's reins to the porch rail and came up the steps, doffing his worn sombrero. He looked from one to the other.

'Evenin', Ma,' he greeted. 'An' to you too, miss. Howdy, Neil.'

'Howdy,' Neil acknowledged, looking up at him in surprise through the haze of his cigarette smoke. 'What's on your mind, Mr Newcomb? This just a social call? We haven't seen you around here for long enough.'

'No, this ain't a social call,' the bearded rancher responded. 'I haven't come clear across fifteen miles just to pass the time of day. Y'see, it's like this.'

He squatted down on the top step, mopped his face with a red kerchief, and then continued, 'I figured I'd like to ask you if you've missed any steers lately from your herd? It's a matter of interest to me.'

Neil frowned and shook his head. 'I guess we haven't, Mr Newcomb. In any case we haven't many steers worth speaking about. Soon know if some went — and none has. Why, what's wrong?'

'Rustlin',' Newcomb said, and his lips tightened. 'There's some low-down dirty rustler at work in this territory. I'm checkin' up on how many people have suffered. So far 'bout five spreads been affected, including my own, and close on five hundred cattle have been stolen . . . ' Newcomb reeled off the names of the ranches concerned, including Naylor's Leaning L. 'I'm goin' into town this evening to put the matter before Sheriff Holton in

Nathan's Cleft. Its time things got looked into.'

Neil whistled. 'Five hundred! Hell, that's plenty!'

'You said it,' the rancher agreed. 'Seems like there's no tellin' where it'll end, or who'll be next. Since you haven't been attacked so far y'might want to keep your eyes skinned.'

'Any rustler I see'll be carryin' a bunch of lilies afore he knows it,' Ma snapped. A thought seemed to strike her. 'You sure about Naylor bein' affected? That jigger might be back of this — he's capable of anythin'!'

'Not this time, Ma. He's suffered too — more than fifty of his cattle were taken. An' that points to a mighty smart rustler. The way Carl's got his spread guarded is sure somethin' to look at — but the cattle have gone just the same.'

'Do him good, anyway,' Ma remarked sourly. Then: 'You'll be stayin' to have a coffee or somethin' after your long ride here?'

Mal Newcomb got to his feet and returned his hat to his head carelessly.

'No thanks, Ma; I'd better be on my way. I want to see how they're goin' on at the Double M and then I aim to be gettin' back to my own place. Plenty to do. Been nice seein' you, folks. 'Night.'

He waved to the responses, and unfastened his mare's reins from the rail. The trio on the porch watched as he went riding into the distance, then Neil turned to look at his mother.

'Ma, since there's rustling going on I reckon you and me and Fleet had best take it in turns to sleep from here on — leastways until the thieves are caught. Any losses from our herd might finish us!'

'What's wrong with me doing a spell of sentry duty, too?' Sylvia frowned.

'You're just not used to it, Syl,' Neil replied. 'You'd probably doze off. Still being pretty new around here the still air knocks you flat, but it won't affect me, Fleet, or Ma in that way.'

'But honestly, I want to — '

'No, Syl, we can't risk it. You get your sleep as usual. We'll stay on the watch.'

So it was decided, in spite of further protests from Sylvia, and a watch was duly kept. For two nights there was no sign of anything unusual occurring, then on the evening of the third night, as they were again taking the evening air on the porch, Neil said:

'I guess I'll have to take up your offer of staying on the watch after all, Syl. I have to go over to Arrowhead Bend this evening to fix a deal,' he explained. 'I won't be back till after midnight, and Fleet will be coming with me. Isn't safe for one man alone to ride the trail after dark when there's a bead on him — as there is on me from Naylor.'

'Leave it to us,' Sylvia said promptly. 'Ma and I will keep things nicely watched.'

'An' we'll sleep in turns, gal,' Ma declared. 'Neil ain't likely to be back afore three in the mornin'. The guy he's dealin' with is a friendly type who likes to talk on into the night over drinks.'

'Just as you say, Ma.' Sylvia gave a smile. 'But I want the first sentry turn, otherwise I mightn't get the chance to do my share.'

5

Death Sentence

After sundown that evening, Ma retired to get her spell of sleep, leaving Sylvia with her .32 in her hand, seated at the living-room window gazing out on to the moonlit expanse. In all the vastness nothing stirred. She caught herself yawning once or twice, weary after her hard day's work in the open air, then forced herself back into wakefulness.

Hours passed and nothing happened. Sylvia yawned again, relaxed a little, and through eyes half-shutting with sleep contemplated the moonlit peace outside. She was not aware of her eyelids closing, but she did know that unexpectedly something hard prodded in her side just above the waistline. It was in that split second that she realized she had been asleep.

'No sound, sister, or I'll blast you,' a man's gravelly voice muttered in her ear. She jerked upright, her heart thudding, and felt frantically for her gun, which had been on the wide window ledge — but it had gone.

'You won't find that gun,' the voice murmured. 'Now stand up and start walkin'. If you try to scream for help I'll drill a hole through your heart . . . Hurry it up!'

Sylvia rose slowly, straining to see who the intruder was. His voice was coarse, uneducated, and one she had never heard before. The man himself was simply a shadowy black figure in the moonlight streaming through the window, a dark kerchief pulled up to his eyes and his black sombrero pulled down nearly to the bridge of his nose.

'Git on your way outside,' he instructed. 'One peep out of you, an' you're dead.'

Sylvia obeyed, and in silence she went out on to the porch, noting as she went that the living-room's second window was pushed wide open — evidence of the intruder's mode of entry. Mentally Sylvia cursed herself for having lapsed into sleep.

As she gained the base of the steps she saw a horse tethered and waiting. Without any words of explanation the gunman moved to her side and lifted her into the saddle. Realizing he had to use both hands to accomplish this Sylvia gave one mighty scream. It ended in a gasp as she was cuffed savagely across the mouth.

She was still recovering from the viciousness of the blow and tasting blood saltily on her tongue when the gunman jolted the horse forward and set off at frantic speed into the moonlight.

Ma, always a light sleeper, awoke with a start at the sound of the scream — then, already fully dressed, she blundered from the bed and snatched at her rifle leaning against the wall. Stumbling to the window she had a brief, shadowy glimpse of a dark, speeding horseman vanishing into the night — and that was all. Muttering lividly to herself she hurried into the adjoining living-room.

As there was no answer to her shouted enquiries, she struck a match and lighted the oil-lamp. Her face grim, she looked about her — then she strode to the open doorway and went out on to the porch. There was only the moonlight and silence.

She went down the steps and stood gazing at the dim signs of a horse's hoofs in the dust, but before she could make a proper attempt to examine them the sound of an approaching rider, or riders, made her pause.

Immediately she withdrew into the shadows and held her rifle in readiness, only to lower it again as she recognized the horsemen as Neil and Fleeting Cloud. Instantly Ma hurried forward.

'The gal's gone!' she snapped, as Neil swung down from the saddle. 'She was on watch whilst I slept — '

'*Gone!* But how — '

'She must've fallen sleep. None of the cattle seems to be missin', but whoever it was came straight into the spread an' took her.'

'I was afraid of this happening! How long ago was this, Ma?'

'No more'n ten minutes. Likely somebody must have bin on the watch, waitin' for a time when you an' Fleet left. Son, I could shoot myself for lettin' the gal take first watch! Guess I'd still be asleep too if she hadn't given a yell as she were carried off. Lookee here! This must be the trail of the cayuse that snatcher was ridin'.'

Neil knelt and examined the ground she indicated. The moonlight was enough for him to see the tracks leading away in the direction of the mountains.

'I guess you're right, Ma.' Neil stood up again. 'But I daren't strike a match to look properly — might be an owl hooter watching somewhere.' He turned to the redskin. 'Here, Fleet, you'd better take a look.' The Indian nodded and squatted down to examine

114

the prints carefully.

'Think you can follow the trail?' Neil asked after a while, and the redskin nodded again, standing up and returning to his horse.

'That settles it,' Ma said. 'Get after her, son, quick as you can. I'll stay awake an' watch in case anythin' else happens here — but it seems to me all the damage has bin done now.'

'OK. See you later, Ma.'

Neil swung from her and vaulted into the saddle. The redskin took the reins of his own horse and, crouching low so that he could follow the trail by the moonlight, led the animal beside him.

Neil chafed at the slowness of progress — though he knew that his own powers of tracking were distinctly inferior to Fleeting Cloud's. To the redskin, tracking was a natural gift bordering on the uncanny, and the bright moonlight helped him considerably. Even when the hoof-prints had lost themselves in the harder, rockier ground at the base of the foothills, the

Indian went on steadily. Pebbles overturned, and subsidences of shingle here and there told their own story to the mute with the eyes of an eagle.

The dawn sky was paling to grey in the east when they reached a narrow cleft leading between two massive spurs of rock. Across the gap had been slung barbed wire secured to stout mesquite posts. Neil, weary of riding and eyes smarting from lack of sleep, dropped from the saddle.

'I don't get it, Fleet,' he said, staring at the barrier. 'This canyon's never been wired off like this before and nobody's got the legal right to do it, either. You're sure the trail led to here?'

The redskin nodded emphatically, so he and Cliff tethered their horses to the nearest mesquite post, eased their way carefully through the midst of the barbed wire, and continued up the narrow cleft. After a dozen yards the Indian caught Neil's arm and stopped him, pointing ahead.

Neil stared incredulously.

In the dim light he could see a mass of cattle moving uneasily in the cramped space. Several beasts lowed mournfully and there came the shift and scrape of animal feet on the loose stones of the canyon floor.

'The rustled cattle!' Neil exclaimed, astounded. 'Someone has used this canyon as a natural corral to pin 'em in — I guess until he's figured out how to get rid of 'em. But where's Syl?' He broke off worriedly, looking about him. 'Anywhere near the feet of these beasts she'd have been trampled to death by now. Let's be — '

The Indian gripped his arm again and pointed to a tall rock some twelve feet above the canyon floor. His abnormally keen eyes had caught something Neil had missed. Gradually Neil realized he was looking at the outlines of a figure lying on top of the spur. Instantly he hurried forward, climbed the rock without difficulty, and breathed a sigh of relief at finding

Sylvia, tightly bound and gagged, striving to free herself. In the space of seconds he had released her and ripped the rag from her teeth.

'Thank God,' she gasped, as he helped her up. 'I was beginning to think that man had left me here to die of thirst, or something! How did — '

'You can thank Fleet for us finding you, Syl. He's an expert at tracking. But who snatched you?'

'No idea, though I'd know his awful voice again if I heard it.'

'Mmm, that may be useful,' Neil decided. 'What happened to you?'

'He brought me here, stuck that filthy rag in my mouth, bound me up, and then went!'

'Doesn't make sense,' Neil frowned deeply. 'Unless it was intended as a kind of warning — Carl Naylor serving notice that he intends to start something. Naturally, he must be at the back of it. But next time we'll be more careful.' Neil glanced about him. 'We'd best be moving. We have to let Sheriff

Holton know about this hidden corral, pronto.'

He helped Sylvia down the rock and they began the return journey to the horses, but before they had gained the barbed-wire barrier figures loomed ahead of them. Instantly Neil's hand flashed down to his gun, only he was a shade too late. A levelled .45 glinted in the moonlight.

'Better not, Neil,' a voice warned sharply. 'You're covered.'

'Sheriff Holton!' Neil exclaimed in surprise. 'I was just aiming to come and get you, Sheriff, to take a look at this corral, and — '

'Am I expected to believe that?' Holton asked grimly.

'Why shouldn't you?' Neil's voice revealed his astonishment at the sheriff's reaction. He looked beyond him to the shadowy figures of the two deputies and behind them to a posse of men.

'Look, Sheriff,' Neil said, as the sheriff remained silent. 'I was going to do you the favour of showing you where all the rustled steers had gone, and — '

'I'm runnin' you in, Neil, together with this redskin sidekick of yourn — and the girl too. If ever there was a neat catch it's this one!'

'Catch?' Neil yelled. 'What the hell you getting at?'

'You don't expect me to believe you came to this secret corral by accident, do you?'

'I came to find Syl — that is, Miss Carfax here. She was snatched, and I tracked her to this place.'

The sheriff gave a grim chuckle. 'Smart of you to manage it in the moonlight where no horse or footprints show in the stones around here.'

'Fleeting Cloud did all the nosing out. You know as well as I do that an Indian can track things down where we're just stone blind.'

'Mebbe . . . but it won't wash, Neil. There's nothing personal in this — we used to be friends. But things are kind of different right now, though. I reckon you're the rustler we've all bin proddin' for this past week or more.'

'That's utterly ridiculous! I tell you that Miss Carfax was kidnapped and that I — '

'You say you followed her, but it so happens that we were tipped off by a *hombre* that he'd seen you, Fleeting Cloud, and this girl all riding together towards this canyon not half an hour ago.'

'Lies!' Neil shouted.

'Is it? It seemed to me a kind of suspicious thing to do at this hour in the morning, so I formed a posse and we rode over for a look-see . . . and I guess I'm quite satisfied with what I've found.'

'I didn't ride here myself,' Sylvia cried angrily. 'I was brought! If I rode here, where's my horse? There isn't one. so — '

'Then what's that?' the sheriff asked cynically. The girl followed his gaze up an acclivity, to where a horse was tied to a mesquite bush, nibbling sparse roots.

'It's not mine!' Sylvia protested, swinging to look at Neil in bewilderment. 'This is Naylor's doing! The man who tipped off the sheriff must have been one of Naylor's men. It might even have been the man who kidnapped me.'

'Could be,' Neil agreed. 'You haven't enough evidence to convict me as a rustler, Sheriff, and you know it!'

'By itself that ain't enough evidence, sure,' Holton agreed, 'but there's other proof that even you can't blink, Neil.'

'What proof?'

'You'll hear about it in court; I'm not wastin' any more time talkin' here. All of you will hear the details soon enough. Now start movin'. You fellers' — he glanced at his men — 'sort out these cattle and find out from their brands where they belong, then ride over and tell the ranchers concerned to come and get their steers back.'

★　★　★

In three separate cells in the little adobe jail at the back of the sheriff's office, Neil, Fleeting Cloud and Sylvia spent the remainder of the night and all next morning — being given a breakfast of sorts — before there were any fresh developments. Then one of Holton's deputies arrived, his keys jangling and a tall, black-suited man trailing behind him.

'Guess you're entitled to have a lawyer defend you, Neil,' the deputy said. 'I dug up Derek Richards to have a word with you.'

Neil nodded to the lanky, slope-shouldered man as he came in. He was middle-aged and balding, with a vinegary face. A worn briefcase was gripped firmly in his right hand and he exuded a general air of business.

''Morning, Neil,' he acknowledged, sitting down on the hard bunk with Neil beside him. 'From all I've been hearing you seem to have gotten yourself nicely tangled up — along with Miss Carfax and Fleeting Cloud.'

'Tangled nothing!' Neil retorted. 'The whole thing's a dirty frame-up, and there could only be one man cunning enough to think it out — Carl Naylor!'

'I'm inclined to agree,' Derek Richards confessed, 'but proving it won't be easy. Naylor's a mighty smart man as I know from past experience — and the prosecutor here is even smarter. The case against you three is so loaded, I don't know if I can break it.'

'Damnit, man, there's no *proof* that I'm the rustler! They can't possibly pin this thing on me without any real evidence.'

'The prosecutor's too smart to rely on circumstantial evidence as his main line,' Richards said.

'Then what else can he rely on? I've not done anything wrong!'

'Mebbe not, but he must have something very sure-fire — and naturally he won't tell me what it is. That'll only spring out in court. All right, I'd better hear your side of it.'

When Neil had finished giving the details of the previous night the lawyer stroked his jaw pensively.

'It's bad,' he muttered. 'The problem is *proof* for your story. There isn't a scrap of it. You say Miss Carfax was kidnapped and — '

'She *was* kidnapped!'

'OK. No doubt she'll confirm it when I talk to her later — but plain words aren't sufficient! Think hard, Neil. What other evidence can you dig up?'

'Well, Ma knows that she was snatched, and — '

'I looked in at your spread on the way here,' Richards interrupted, 'and your Ma told me the same story. Believe me, feller, she raised blue hell! Mebbe she'll be over here soon to see you . . . '

'Very probably, or I don't know Ma. But surely you got something from her you can use?'

'She told me that she only saw a smudge vanishing into the night and then discovered that the girl had gone.

That doesn't prove anything. On the other hand the sheriff was tipped off by a saddle tramp who says he saw you, Fleeting Cloud and the girl riding together — '

'Whoever the *hombre* was that told that story was lying!'

'Mebbe he was, Neil, but the trouble is his story will likely carry more weight with a jury. Add to that some other evidence of which we know nothing until the trial, and the fact that Holton found you all at the corral — and with three horses there — then the position begins to look mighty ugly.'

'Just how ugly?' Neil asked quietly.

'Rustling is a hanging offence in this territory.' Derek Richards turned grim eyes to Neil's sombre face. 'You and that Indian are liable to be guests of honour at a necktie party unless we can think of something convincing.'

'What about Sylvia?'

'My guess is that she'll be cited as an accessory only — but she'll certainly get some kind of punishment.'

Neil breathed hard and beat his fists impotently on the bunk beside him.

'If only we could pin something on Naylor! He's obviously behind all this! He vowed he'd get even after Fleet and I beat him up, and this is his low-down way of doing it without facing me man to man.'

'We'll take that for granted,' Richards said. 'But you can be mighty sure he won't have done anything that can be traced back to him.'

'Then what do we do?'

'There's nothing you can do, Neil.' The lawyer got to his feet. 'You're stuck here and will remain — like Miss Carfax and the Indian. 'I'll do the best I can for you, but we'll have to hope something new in the way of evidence turns up.'

After the lawyer had taken his departure, looking distinctly morose, Neil was left to fume over the cunning fashion in which he had been framed.

About an hour later Ma arrived and her language was a revelation that could be heard all over the jail and the sheriff's office. Not that it made a scrap of difference.

Inexorably two more days and nights passed . . . and then the trial was convened.

When the three accused were led into the dock on the fateful morning they found the courtroom packed out. Court sessions were rare in Nathan's Cleft — not through any lack of crime, but because the guilty ones were rarely caught, or else things were settled by gun law. This one had the added attraction of seeing a rustler and his accomplices get their deserts.

That most people knew Neil had led a straight, hard-working life up to now counted for nothing with the cynical men of the town. The womenfolk had Sylvia in their blackest books, convinced that but for her Neil would never have turned to crime anyway.

Only one thing seemed to be in their favour, and this was that Judge Garvice was presiding. A good lawyer, he was also renowned in the district for his sense of justice, and if any evidence was presented which did not measure up to his standards it would be promptly thrown out.

So the trial began.

As Neil listened stonily to the recital of facts gathered against himself and the others, he looked about the court-room. In the distance he could see Carl Naylor on a corner chair, smiling in grim satisfaction, whilst in the front row sat his mother, her arms folded, face dogged, giving an encouraging glance every now and again.

The first witness the prosecution called was a ragged, unshaven cow-puncher. He took the oath and then calmly repeated the statement he had already made: that he had seen Neil, Sylvia and Fleeting Cloud all riding together in the early hours of the morning in the direction of the canyon corral.

'It's lies, Judge!' Neil shouted, unable to contain himself and banging his fist on the dock rail. 'I never saw this tramp in my life before — and so how did he recognize me? And Fleeting Cloud was not riding! He was walking alongside his horse and examining the trail as he went — '

'You'll have a chance to speak your piece later,' Judge Garvice interrupted, peering over steel-rimmed spectacles. 'And until then you'd better keep quiet!'

Neil scowled, then at a warning look from Richards he relaxed. The prosecutor swung again on the witness.

'You are perfectly sure you saw the three prisoners riding in the manner stated?' he demanded. 'At what time was this?'

'Yes sir, I sure did. I was a-ridin' the trail into Nathan's Cleft in the small hours of the mornin' and that was when I saw 'em. The moon was up so I saw 'em clearly enough.'

'And it was then that you decided to tell the sheriff what you had seen?'

'Sure.'

The prosecutor nodded, satisfied. 'Your witness,' he said briefly, and returned to his desk to inspect his papers.

Derek Richards got up slowly, hands in pockets as he drifted over to where the saddle tramp stood on the witness stand.

'What made you decide to tell the sheriff what you'd seen? You surely could not have judged from their behaviour in simply being out riding that they were up to anything suspicious?'

'I — I guess I'd heard about the rustlin' in this territory an' — '

'Who told told you?' Richards snapped.

'I — er — well, folks generally.'

'Not very convincing,' Richards observed sourly. 'You are unknown in this district and yet you would have us believe you have been around long enough to hear general gossip . . . Well, carry on with your story.'

'I figured that three riders at that

hour in the mornin' headed for the foothills — an' without bedrolls — was mighty suspicious. So I thought it my dooty to tell the sheriff about it.'

'Your sudden desire to do your duty is at the least extraordinary, my friend . . . ' Richards smiled cynically and turned to look at Sylvia.

'Miss Carfax, would you say that this is the man who kidnapped you in the first instance?'

'As far as I can tell, no,' Sylvia answered. 'I don't recognize his voice.'

'I see. Thank you.' Richards tightened his lips, dismissed the witness, and then returned to his desk to brood.

Ma Grantham was the next to come to the stand, but beyond a forceful account of how she had been asleep when the abduction of Sylvia had occurred she had nothing material to add which could be considered useful evidence. Sylvia herself was not called, because Richards had adjudged that if the prosecutor got her on the stand, by clever questioning he could build up a

132

powerful motive for Neil's alleged crimes.

Then came the sheriff — heavy, impersonal, taking the oath with an air of long accustomedness.

The prosecutor played his trump card.

'On the face of it, Sheriff, it would appear that the prisoners were arrested on more or less circumstantial evidence and the guesswork of a lone rider passing through the district. That, of course, would never suffice for this court. But I understand that you have something more concrete to offer in regard to the matter?'

'I sure have,' Holton declared, glancing about him in obvious triumph. 'I'd known for some time that Neil Grantham was the man we wanted, but I was waitin' for a chance to find out where the stolen cattle had gone — an' that chance came when the lone rider tipped me off. *I'd found the hoof-marks of Neil's sorrel at each ranch where the cattle was stolen from!*'

This revelation brought a murmur of conversation that quickly went round the courtroom. The judge's gavel descended sharply and restored quiet. Derek Richards jerked up his head from his notes as he realized he had come face to face with the masterstroke he had been anticipating.

'Most horse's hoof-marks look alike, don't they?' the prosecutor asked. 'What made you so sure they belonged to Grantham's mount?'

'I took a cast of 'em and compared 'em with his horse one night. That was some time ago when the rustlin' first began. Those in his ranch didn't know anythin' about it — I waited my chance until I judged they'd be asleep.'

'I still do not consider that this is positive evidence.' the judge commented.

'But it is, your Honour!' the sheriff insisted. 'That shoe on the left foreleg of Grantham's horse is put on crooked because of a callus on the animal's foot. When I first looked for evidence of the rustler at the ranches I noticed this crooked shoe-mark kept coming up every time . . . '

The judge listened intently and presently his eyes strayed to Neil as he stood gripping the dock rail, his eyes bright and hard with incredulity.

'So, your Honour,' the sheriff continued, 'the next thing I did was see the blacksmith in Nathan's Cleft here, and he told me he only knew of one horse with a shoe crosswise like that, specially made crooked, and that was Neil Grantham's. So I made my comparisons and got my evidence. When I got the news that the accused were all headed to that canyon I figured it might be the finishing touch — and it was, since we found the cattle all nicely tied up.'

'Thanks, Sheriff' the prosecutor said, a gleam in his eyes. 'Your witness,' he added to Richards, who got to his feet.

'I've no questions to ask the sheriff, Your Honour, but I would like permission to put Neil Grantham on the stand.'

'Granted.'

Richards regarded Neil as he finished the oath and stood gripping the rail.

'You have heard what the prosecution has had to say. What is your own version of it, Neil? Can you explain how the prints of your sorrel could possibly have gotten to the various ranches which have been robbed?'

'No, I can't,' Neil admitted grimly. 'All l can tell you is I never rode to any of the ranches.'

'Do you think it possible that anybody else might have done so, by night, on your horse?'

'I'd say that it's most unlikely — particularly with Fleeting Cloud prowling about by night watching for intruders, as he often is. Another thing: my horse is trained to whinny out loud if anybody but me tries to ride him. Had that happened, we'd have heard something. I'm willing to swear my horse never moved from the stable without my knowing about it.'

'Do you realize, feller, that you're

making things tough for me, and even tougher for yourself?' Richards sighed. 'Then how d'you explain the shoe-prints?'

'I just don't know,' Neil said bitterly, 'but I know who does! Carl Naylor, sitting grinning over there! He's engineered this whole thing from start to finish, and if anybody can explain it, he can. Why don't you start asking him a few — '

'You will confine yourself to answering questions,' the judge interrupted.

'I haven't any more, Your Honour,' Richards sighed. 'I guess the prosecution has cut the ground from under my feet — and now Neil is making it a durned sight worse. I don't see there's anything more I can do with it.'

Disgusted, he returned to his desk and sat glowering. Neil gave him a somewhat helpless look and then turned as he was escorted back to the dock.

The final witness was the blacksmith who testified to the fact that he had fitted the oblique shoe on Neil's sorrel — which made it that, in putting down its front feet, the horse had one shoe-print at an angle to its fellow.

The blacksmith dismissed, the prosecutor and then Derek Richards made their final addresses to the jury. This completed, Judge Garvice looked at the jurymen thoughtfully.

'You have heard the evidence,' he said, 'and it is now up to you to come to a verdict. To do this you will also bear in mind the earlier statements of the prosecutor in which he showed that Neil Grantham is a poor rancher struggling hard to improve his business since the arrival of Miss Carfax. Men have lost their sense of proportion in the past when there has been the need to impress women and obtain money. On the other hand, you must remember Neil Grantham's record up to the time of the rustlings. There wasn't a harder, more upright worker in this territory ... Now you may retire.'

The jury straggled out and the accused were led back to the tiny detention room. Only ten minutes later they were recalled. The reassembled court waited tensely as, questioned by Judge Garvice, the foreman spoke up.

'We find Neil Grantham and Fleeting Cloud both guilty of cattle-stealing, Your Honour, and Miss Carfax as an accessory, without perhaps being an active participant in the crimes. Being from New Orleans and also inexperienced with cattle, we can't agree that she would be connected with any actual cattle-stealing.'

The judge nodded, looked at Neil through his spectacles for a long moment, and then said:

'You have heard the verdict. Have you anything further to say before I pass sentence?'

'Only that the whole thing's a dirty, low-down frame-up, Your Honour — and also I think you're hogtied like the rest of us, and because of that not able to use your own judgement.'

'In this territory.' the judge contin-ued, 'the punishment for cattle-thieving is death by hanging — and that is the sentence which must be carried out at dawn tomorrow, upon you, Neil Grantham, and you, Fleeting Cloud. As an accessory, Miss Carfax, I am empowered to order you to leave this territory within six hours and never return to it, otherwise you will be imprisoned for — '

'*A moment, Judge!*' a voice exclaimed, and Carl Naylor came swiftly up the courtroom, and approached the judge's desk.

'Well, Mr Naylor?' Garvice asked coldly. 'Please make it brief.'

'In regard to Miss Carfax, your Honour, the law grants that if some-body stands surety in a certain amount for her good behaviour she can stay in the territory. So my lawyer has been telling me, anyway.'

'Correct,' the judge agreed, making no effort to disguise his inner feelings towards the saloon-owner.

'Then with the court's permission,' Naylor said, 'I would like to stand surety for Miss Carfax, in whatever sum may be named.'

'I am not in a position to refuse the offer,' Garvice replied, 'but the prisoner has the right to say whether she prefers this redemption to the alternative of leaving the district. It is up to you, Miss Carfax.'

As Sylvia hesitated, Ma Grantham sprang to her feet in the front row.

'Don't you be a-takin' any heed of this low-down skunk, gal!' she cried, waving her fists. 'You're better leavin' altogether than bein' under the thumb of this dirty no-good!'

'Ma Grantham's biased, Judge,' Naylor explained drily, turning to the judge. As Garvice said nothing, his grin faded a little and he continued:

'I can assure you, Judge — and you, Miss Carfax — that my intentions are quite honourable and — '

'Hah!' Ma scoffed. 'If this wasn't a courtroom I'd spit good an' hard in your face, Carl Naylor!'

The gavel banged savagely.

'Take it easy, Mrs Grantham!' the judge cautioned. Ma shrugged, and then waited.

'My intentions,' Naylor repeated, 'are honourable. In the past I behaved badly towards Miss Carfax and I'd like to make amends. If I stand surety for her there are no strings attached. It simply means she will be free, and that if she breaks the law in any way I'll be hauled up to answer for it. Up to you, Miss Carfax,' he added, looking at her with his keen dark eyes.

'Very well, I accept the offer,' Sylvia agreed, after a brief hesitation.

'Knowing that I am to be hanged, have you no more guts than to let this gorilla buy your freedom?' Neil whispered, staring at her.

'If you have any truck with this critter, gal, you can keep away from the Blue Circle for all time!' Ma yelled angrily.

'I've made my decision,' Sylvia

declared, colouring.

'But, Syl — ' Neil could not proceed any further. He was seized and dragged away, Fleeting Cloud beside him.

'See the clerk about the surety money, Mr Naylor,' Judge Garvice ordered curtly. 'The court is dismissed.'

6

Sylvia Takes a Hand

Half an hour later Sylvia left the courthouse, with her possessions returned to her. She had Carl Naylor beside her, but her memory was of the contemptuous eyes of Neil and the earthy scorn of Ma Grantham as she had marched off in disgust.

Sylvia came to a stop on the sunny boardwalk and looked up at the saloon owner's smiling features.

'I just can't believe that you've freed me and intend to let it go at that. What do you want of me besides?'

Carl grinned. 'You may not credit it, but I've actually got a conscience. That surety money was just a penance payment for the other night. I should have known better — that you're not that kind of a girl.'

Sylvia considered him. 'Well, that being so, all I can say is thanks for helping me.'

'Pleasure. What are you going to do now? With things so unhealthy for Neil in the future your outlook seems hazy to me.'

'Which no doubt pleases you a lot! Neil condemned to death — and actually innocent of any real crime — and I am more or less under your thumb.'

Carl shrugged. 'Think that of me if you like. But I was asking you — what are you planning to do next?'

'Find somewhere to stay whilst I think things out. Ma made it pretty plain that the Blue Circle's off limits to me.' Sylvia studied the high street absently. At length, she nodded to a big rooming-house across the road. 'I'll stop over there for a while. Later I'll go back to the Blue Circle and get the rest of my things.'

'OK. You can always find me either at the Lucky Chance or my Leaning L ranch at Cragpoint. If you decide to blow town after all, let me know: I might be able to recover some of the surety money.'

Carl raised his semi-clerical hat and then went on his way. Sylvia stared after him, danger lights smouldering in her grey-blue eyes. Then she walked to the rooming-house across the street and had no difficulty in securing a room on the top floor.

Once in her room she locked the door, went across to the bed, and lay on it to think. She continued to do so, with breaks only for meals, until the evening. By this time she had made up her mind.

Her only objective now was to somehow save Neil and Fleeting Cloud from the hangman's rope on the morrow. That Neil probably now despised her did not matter. She had a job to do — to save two innocent men — and for perhaps the first time in her life everything was planted firmly on her own shoulders.

Towards sundown she freshened up as well as she could, and then went across the street to the corner drugstore. Here she made a special purchase and afterwards continued on her way to the Lucky Chance. It was at the height of the evening's business, with Naylor in the smoky distance leaning against one of the ornate pillars, a cheroot in the corner of his big mouth.

From her position by the batwings Sylvia contemplated him for a moment, then as her eyes strayed to a corner she gave a start of surprise.

Ma Grantham was seated at a table with a glass of beer in front of her and a small group of punchers gathered on either side of her. Beyond thinking it queer behaviour for a mother about to lose her son at a hanging party, Sylvia gave her no more attention.

She knew Ma had seen her, for out of the tail of her eye she caught the old woman's stony glance. Affecting not to notice, Sylvia finished her journey to stand beside Carl Naylor.

147

He looked at her and grinned, removing his cheroot from his mouth with his bandaged hand.

'Well, what gives?' he enquired.

'Could we go to your private room?'

'Huh?' He looked at the girl blankly. 'You mean you're willing to take the chance after what happened before?'

Sylvia considered him with a level gaze. 'You atoned for that by bailing me out, and I'm sure you won't dare attempt the same thing again.'

'You've got many qualities, Syl — and not least nerve!' Carl declared in admiration. 'Mebbe that's what I like about you.'

Sylvia waited, and in the distance she could descry Ma Grantham still staring at her fixedly. Then Carl jerked his head. She preceded him into the private room. Her calm, off-hand manner belied the fact that her heart was hammering fiercely enough to choke her.

'Care to risk another drink?' he asked, smiling crookedly.

148

'Why not? Provided it's straight brandy with no soda and no doctoring.' Sylvia sat down at the table as he lit the oil-lamp. 'I can drink with any man when there are no drugs added.'

'OK,' Carl admitted, 'So I drugged the last drink you had. I was a bad boy. But never again! A straight brandy it is — with a man to drink beside you. I guess I can easily match anything you can do.'

As he turned to the doorway Sylvia removed from the pocket of her jodhpurs the purchase she had made at the drug store. It was a small phial marked PURE ALCOHOL which she had bought ostensibly for cleaning her begrimed clothes. After removing the cork, she kept the phial in her left palm, her thumb over the neck, and waited for Carl to return to the table.

He proffered cigarettes in his gold case, and though she had given up smoking Sylvia took one of the weeds and allowed smoke to trickle from her nostrils after he had lighted it for her. It tasted dry and unpleasant and she wondered vaguely why she had ever liked the beastly things.

'Naturally,' Carl said, sitting down, 'you must have some reason for risking being alone with me again.'

'Of course — but if you don't mind I'll have a drink before I start explaining.'

The drinks were not long in coming. This time Carl did not get up and lock the door after the waiter had departed. He pushed Sylvia's filled glass over to her and then contemplated the brandy's deep amber colouring.

'Would it surprise you to know,' Sylvia asked, looking into his eyes, 'that in spite of all that has happened I'm very much in love with you?'

'Sure it would,' he assented drily. 'I've given you no reason to like me.'

'How do you know? I came to you the other night because I wanted you as a friend. You drugged my brandy and soda and knocked the senses out of me. That's all I remember. The rest Neil told me. Just the same, Carl, I still want to know you better. In every way you can give me so much more than Neil has ever done. I don't hold that drugging act against you. The kind of girl I am you can have all you want without resorting to that.'

Carl looked at her fixedly — the clearness of her grey-blue eyes, the firmness of her mouth. With his immense conceitedness, he found it impossible to entirely disbelieve what she had said.

'Say, mebbe I've had you figured wrong from the start,' he mused. 'I thought you'd be dead against me after what happened.'

'Not a bit. In fact I think that I've had a pretty merciful release from Neil and Ma Grantham. They're not my class, groping away on that cabbage patch. Not that Neil will grope much longer, anyway.'

As she talked Sylvia lowered her cigarette so that it finished just under the table's edge. Deliberately she crushed the glowing end of it on the woodwork, out of sight; then returning the cigarette to her lips as she finished speaking she dragged at it uselessly.

'Match, Carl,' she requested. 'This has gone dead on me.'

He reached forward and struck a match in his cupped hands. As the flame began to dance Sylvia blew through her nostrils and extinguished the glow. Below the table's edge the phial of alcohol was still in her left hand. Carl tried again with another match and as he did so her left hand stole under his leaning body. He never saw the action, and by the time he'd relit the cigarette the alcohol phial was empty, its contents in Carl's brandy.

'So there it is.' Sylvia sat back and smiled. 'You and I . . . Why don't we have a drink on it, and then I'll tell you more?'

Carl smiled back, and raised his glass. The expression on his face still showed bewilderment at her frank attitude. Like most men of the region he did not sip or taste his drink — a factor upon which Sylvia was banking. He drank the contents at a clean gulp and then sat pondering.

'Tastes sort of flat,' he commented, licking his lips. 'Better get yours drunk, Syl. Mebbe we left the stuff too long.'

Sylvia sipped at her own drink, taking care to swallow only the minutest quantity of spirit; she needed a clear head. She gave the impression of drinking slowly but consistently, her eyes watching Carl intently all the time through her lashes.

After a while Naylor straightened up, and there was a visible effort in his movements.

'I'm still waiting — you were going to tell me more,' he said thickly.

'In a moment,' Sylvia responded, still stalling for time.

'What difference — dussit make? No reason why — why we can't talk now, iser?' Carl blinked and rubbed his face slowly; then he started muttering to himself. 'I guess I — I oughta pin that barkeep's ears back for servin' bad brandy . . . ' He swayed giddily forward for a moment then straightened again, obviously bemused and astonished at his lapse.

Then his dark eyes narrowed as Sylvia suddenly got to her feet. She came round the table swiftly and before his stupid movements could prevent her she had yanked the big Colt revolver with the pearl-inlaid butt from its holster. She pointed the heavy gun directly at his face.

'Now it's my turn, Carl,' she said coldly, looking down on him. 'You drank brandy — and pure alcohol! Being colourless you didn't notice it. I hope it chokes you! You're about due any moment for the worst hangover you've ever had!'

'What's — what's th' idea?' Carl slurred, staring at her blearily. 'I said I was sorry I did it you — an' I didn't use al'col on you — used sump'n else . . . ' He grinned foolishly.

Sylvia half-perched herself on the

154

table, the gun pointing steadily. 'I'm here tonight for only one thing, Carl — to get the truth out of you. As I calculated, you're becoming intoxicated. Before long you'll be talking about all kinds of things — and when you get that far I'm calling in witnesses to listen to you. I mean to get at the facts concerning how you framed Neil.'

'You crazy bitch . . . '

Carl made a wild lunge but Sylvia drew back warily. He finished up with his forearms on the table and his head lolling on them. Sylvia waited, her whole attention concentrated for a moment when he might lose control and start talking aimlessly as the alcohol released his tongue.

After a long pause Carl began mumbling to himself and Sylvia relaxed a little. He seemed to be half-asleep and his words were unintelligible. Sylvia leaned closer to hear him — and this was where she underestimated him.

His hands suddenly flashed up and seized upon her slender throat, crushing

155

with terrifying power. The fact that his right palm was bandaged did not prevent him using all the strength of his fingers. With a tremendous effort Sylvia twisted in his grip and slammed the gun butt down towards his head. It struck his shoulder instead, but it did have the effect of dislodging his hold.

Instantly she sprang free but he grabbed the gun from her at the last moment.

'OK,' he said bitterly, swaying to his feet. 'So you thought I was the kind of lily who'd wilt under alcohol, did you? You forgot one thing, Syl. I'm a — a hardened drinker! Nice little playmate, ain't you?' he breathed.

Sylvia remained by the further wall, watching him narrowly and measuring her distance to the door, ready to fling herself towards it if things became dangerous.

'Y' know something? I jus' thought of a good way to pay you back — tell you everythin' an' make it so's you can do nothin' about it! Serve you right, huh?'

Sylvia gazed at him steadily as he swayed again. 'With nobody t'listen to me except you it won't mean a thing! Good, eh?'

As Sylvia made a slight movement he brought the gun up sharply.

'But I can always take a shorter cut an' put a bullet through your fancy hide,' Carl warned. 'Come over here beside me, where I can watch what you're doin'.'

Slowly Sylvia moved to the table where she had formerly been seated, pushing aside the still almost-full glass of brandy at her elbow. She considered it for a moment, then turned her eyes back to Carl.

He sat down heavily, fighting hard to keep his senses, his gun resting on the edge of the table so that its muzzle directly faced her.

'Yeah — sure I framed Neil an' that dirty dumb Indian. Why not? He beat me up and that redskin put a knife through my hand. It's gettin' better now but it's been givin' me hell . . . '

Carl paused to rub his forehead before continuing:

'I've known for a long time, same as most folk around here, that Neil's horse has a specially made crooked shoe. When he came here to rescue you he left nice clear horse prints in the dirt outside — an' that gave me the idea. I had the blacksmith come over next day, make a cast of it, and then fashion an identical shoe. Clever, eh?'

Sylvia listened intently to these revelations, bitterly regretful of the fact that nobody else was present as a witness.

'Naturally,' Carl grinned, 'the blacksmith won't say anythin'. He knows what's good for his health! One word outa place an' he'd be a dead pigeon. Well, my boys started rustlin' cattle an' packin' 'em in that canyon — and each time prints of a crooked shoe were left behind. When the ranchers started complainin' to the sheriff I made the final move. I detailed one of my boys to keep watch on the Blue Circle and be sure of a time when you an' Ma Grantham would be left alone. I knew he'd go to Arrowhead Bend on business eventually — an' he did. That's when you were snatched.'

'Just the sort of filthy trick you'd pull,' Sylvia commented sourly. She tensed as Naylor swayed slightly. But he gripped the table tightly and regained his balance with an effort.

'I also knew that that Indian would track you down so I had my puncher leave a good trail to follow. Another man — that *hombre* who tipped off the sheriff — was posted to watch if the Indian an' Neil managed to track you down,' he continued. 'If he didn't, there was another plan waitin' to be put into action. I roped that saddle tramp in from another town so's he couldn't be known around here. When he *did* see Neil an' the Indian lookin' for you he told the sheriff. That gullible fool was jus' in time to nab th' whole bunch of you . . . '

'Very smart,' Sylvia said acidly. 'But it

shows you just didn't have the guts to come out into the open and shoot it out with Neil, doesn't it?'

'Only a fool exposes himself to danger when there's a safer way. I guess I still had several uneasy moments. Once Holton had found those crooked prints he was all for nailin' Neil right then — but I needed to get that redskin an' you roped in too. So when all the ranchers who'd had cattle stolen went to his office for a conference I said we should wait 'til the time when Neil led us to where the cattle might be hidden — an' that fool Holton went for the idea. Since some of my cattle had gone too, nobody suspected me.'

Sylvia said nothing, but her hand closed round the glass of brandy close by.

'So there it is,' Carl finished, flattening his palms on the table and leaning forward intently. 'As neat a job of hogtyin' as any you came across. In one fell swoop, it settled Neil, that filthy redskin — an' you!'

Sylvia sat looking at him in stony contempt, although at the back of her mind she was marvelling at his strength in resisting the power of the pure alcohol — and to her dismay he actually seemed to be recovering as he got to his feet.

'I'm getting quite a kick out of this,' he said drily. 'I've told you everything, but there's nothing y'can do about it without a witness, and I'll never make the confession again. I've got Neil and that redskin out of the way and I've got you answerable to me for good behaviour. You didn't think I really stood surety for you just because I felt generous, did you?'

'You didn't think *I* meant it when I said I loved you, did you?' Sylvia snapped.

Silence. They looked at each other.

'So I guess that makes us even,' Carl said at last. 'The way I figure things you won't blow town as long as you think there's a chance of proving Neil innocent. Even if he's been hung you'll

161

stick around, if only to try and prove that he died without cause and to bring the real crook to justice. Meaning me, of course.' He paused and gave a leering grin.

'That suits me fine! I've made up my mind you're the gal I want for a wife before I'm through. The fact that we don't love each other doesn't matter. You've got the looks that I like in a woman. To my mind there just isn't any other rule to go by.'

'You low-down contemptible beast,' Sylvia whispered, getting slowly to her feet also. 'Never in my life have I — '

Suddenly Sylvia whipped up her brandy from the table and dashed the spirit straight into his face. He gasped and dropped his gun as both hands clapped to his eyes, the stinging liquid blinding him for a moment.

It was enough for Sylvia. As he cursed and groped around she hurtled to the door, snatched it open, then lunged into the haze and confusion of the saloon. She had a brief glimpse of the men and women at the tables staring at her, including Ma Grantham, as she blundered through their midst.

Then she had plunged through the batwings and into the clear night air.

Swiftly she reviewed her position. With Ma Grantham still in the Lucky Chance it seemed as good a time as any to go over to the Blue Circle, get her belongings, and then come back to the boarding-house and perhaps think up some new strategy before dawn.

She crossed the street to the livery stable, hired out a mare, and then rode the trail under the night sky to the Blue Circle. As she had expected, the ranch was locked up but the window of her own room was partly open at the top. In a few minutes, leaving her mare tethered to the gate, she had opened one of the windows to the full and scrambled into the dark room beyond.

To collect her belongings took some time, particularly as in the first instance she had brought a cabin trunk and suitcase. She had packed them both to capacity and was considering them in the light of the oil-lamp when a slight sound made her turn sharply. The bedroom door opened and a grim-faced Ma Grantham stood in the shadowy aperture.

'I thought I told you never to come here again!' As she came forward, the lamplight showed her face to be hard and pitiless, her eyes glinting.

'I'm only here to collect my things, Ma,' Sylvia explained, and turned away.

'Then collect 'em quick and git out!'

As Sylvia hesitated, Ma seized her arm and shook it violently.

'I said git out, gal! Buyin' yourself out of court the way you did, an' then sidin' with that skunk Naylor — an' with Neil due for a necktie party tomorrow! For all your fancy city ways, I reckon your morals just plain stink!'

Sylvia snatched her arm away angrily.

'I didn't notice that you seemed particularly concerned in the saloon, Ma! Drinking beer and chatting with those down-at-heel punchers! Not exactly the sorrow-stricken mother, were you?'

'I had my reasons for bein' there,' Ma retorted. 'An' I sure know what your reasons were! I don't need no imagination to guess what went on in Naylor's back room. He came out after you, ragin' drunk, an' the things he said left no doubt as what you had bin up to with him. I thought when you first came here you'd make a good wife for my son, but now I know you're nothin' but a no-good, an' somehow it always stinks worse in a woman than a man. Man's got it in his nature; a woman only gits that way through circumstances or because she plain wants to an' I reckon in your case it ain't circumstances.'

Sylvia smarted under the verbal tirade, wondering if she ought to explain her real reasons for her actions. Then she tightened her lips.

'I'm going,' she said quietly, and there was something in her tone that brought a momentary puzzled look to Ma's face. 'I'll have somebody come over and collect this cabin trunk tomorrow. All I can manage tonight is the suitcase so I'll — '

'You'll find the blasted trunk on the trail outside the yard gates!' Ma snapped. 'I want no stuff of yourn left in the place. Now git movin'!'

Sylvia went without another word. Ma came behind her, the cabin trunk on her shoulder, her powerful frame hardly staggering under the weight. When she had crossed the yard and reached the open gateway she dumped the trunk in the dust, turned back, and slammed the gates. Sylvia, in the road beyond them, stood looking after her in the moonlight.

A new mood swayed her. She had never yet accomplished anything in her life of her own free will: inevitably she had fallen back on somebody else to help her. She had one last chance to redeem her uselessness. If she happened to succeed explanations would be unnecessary: the act would speak for itself. If she failed it would not matter

166

anyway, and she would have to quit town and return to New Orleans.

Thus decided, she heaved the suitcase up to the back of her hired mare, secured it there, then vaulted into the saddle. In fifteen minutes she was back in Nathan's Cleft. The town was quiet now, its lights extinguished. The rowdiness of the Lucky Chance had subsided, its habitués having departed to their homesteads and bunkhouses.

Sylvia left her mare at the night-and-day livery stable and then returned to her room in the rooming-house. Wearied, she sat down on the bed to think. She did not bother to light the oil-lamp as moonlight filled the room. It was 2 a.m. — only about five hours left until dawn. If she was to save Neil it meant that she would have to make a masterstroke in that time.

Relaxing on the bed she set herself to think, going back over all she had accomplished so far. She now knew Naylor's guilt for certain, but the problem was to prove it, or make him repeat his confession in the presence of witnesses.

From now on he would be wary of her, and would remain so even after the hanging of Neil and Fleeting Cloud had taken place. With him ruled out, therefore, there had to be some other way — an indirect one — of proving what he had admitted to her. Perhaps the blacksmith could be made to admit that he had cast a crooked shoe to Carl's order? Most unlikely. He'd have been heavily bribed to keep his mouth shut and his fear of reprisal would make him deny all knowledge of the affair.

Perhaps, then, there might be some evidence somewhere to show that Naylor had paid certain of his men to do the rustling jobs? A payroll check-sheet perhaps?

Or there might even be a receipted bill for the work done by the blacksmith? Such a bill, brought to the notice of the sheriff, would make a starting point for a further investigation and postpone the hanging. There were only two places where such a receipt might conceivably be — either in Carl's office in the saloon, or at his ranch.

To attempt to enter his ranch would be too dangerous a proposition, but the Lucky Chance was definitely a good risk. Sylvia got up from the bed quickly and looked through the window at the saloon across the street. It lay deserted in the bright moonlight.

She made up her mind and gently drew up the lower sash of the window, easing herself out on to the sloping roof of the front porch. It was better to go this way to avoid possible awkward questions from awakened boarders or the hotel's owner.

She reached the bottom of the sloping roof and scrambled over the gutter, slid down one of the main pillars, and so gained the street. Swiftly as a shadow she crossed over and gained the welcome protection of the gloom of the boardwalk on the opposite side.

As she had expected, the main doors

were securely locked, so she glided round the side of the big wooden edifice and investigated until she found a window with a frosted-glass pane. It was of the ordinary top-and-bottom sash variety. Having no penknife the only article she could use was the pin of her brooch.

It bent under the strain but finally forced back the fairly loose catch. Sylvia paused once more, refastening the brooch in her kerchief — none too securely after its maltreatment — and glanced around her. Satisfied that everywhere was still quiet she raised the sash, hauled herself up, then half-fell into the room beyond. Quickly she steadied herself and closed the window after her.

She waited, accustoming her eyes to the deep gloom of the room. The moonlight was diffused by the frosted glass, but its pale grey glow enabled her to recognize a roll-top desk, a safe, a table stacked with box files, one or two chairs . . . It was evidently the office, the very place she wanted.

She began groping around again until she came to the oil-lamp. Beside it, as was customary, there was a box of matches. She had no intention of lighting the lamp and giving away her presence: all she needed was a match-glimmer, well cupped in her hands, to give her some idea of what she was doing.

She picked up the box, moved to the roll-top desk and heaved at it. It was securely locked, which meant that imevitably its drawers were as well. Irritated, she turned to the safe, and finding this an even more formidable proposition, she moved on to the files.

Unable to read the writing on the labels she struck one of the matches. The file marked 'Miscellaneous Accounts' looked as if it might prove promising.

She laid it on the table, opened it and began to search, striking innumerable matches and then shielding each one. She became impatient at the wealth of irrelevant receipts and bills she encountered, none of which showed the least sign of being of use to her.

Suddenly what seemed like a tremendous explosion made her jump and set her heart racing painfully. Then as she realized it had been the report of a gun, the door, its lock shattered by a bullet, suddenly slammed wide open and a shadowy figure stood in the gloomy rectangle, the grey abyss of the pool-room behind.

'All right, sister, take it easy,' the intruder said coldly. 'Git over here!'

7

The Escape

As Sylvia remained motionless, her slender figure silhouetted against the moonlight on the frosted-glass window, the intruder came forward with the light glinting on his gun barrel. A match flared as he struck it down his pants, and, one-handedly, lighted the oil-lamp.

Sylvia found herself looking at a swarthy, weather-beaten face with a day's stubble marring the hard jaw line. Here, she knew, was the man who had first kidnapped her! She had already recognized the gravelly voice from the few words he had spoken.

'Snooping around, huh?' he asked grimly, considering her.

'Right!' Sylvia agreed boldly.

'Mebbe you'd have gotten away with it, too, but you were a little too handy with them matches! My room's just across the street, and I was just unlacing my boots before hittin' the hay when I saw through the window the flare of a match in this office here. Mighty good job I did, too. I reckon prowlers ain't so welcome around here.'

'Meaning that Carl Naylor is your boss?' Sylvia asked.

'Sure he is. I'm his right-hand man. That's why I had a key to the outside door. Rocky Campbell's the name.' There was a note of pride in the uneducated voice.

'Right-hand gunman, you mean,' Sylvia commented with contempt. 'I suppose you're going to shoot me now? An unarmed woman?'

'Sassy dame, ain't you,' Campbell remarked sourly. 'I'd sure like to plug you after that crack, but I ain't takin' the risk. Nope — I aim to run you in to the boss an' see what he sez. Now git outa here an' don't try anythin' funny!'

They passed through the doorway and into the big, dark saloon about which there still hung the obnoxious odour of stale liquor and tobacco smoke. She opened the Yale-locked door beyond the batwings. Rocky Campbell came steadily behind her, following her out to the boardwalk.

'Keep movin'!' he snapped, as she halted. 'I've my cayuse to git to take us out to the boss's spread.'

As the gun jabbed in her back Sylvia went obediently across the street. She knew she had no alternative other than to obey the gun-hawk's orders. And there was the glimmering of an idea at the back of her mind. If she played her cards aright there was just a chance that she might be able to turn this fresh defeat into a victory.

Keeping the girl covered, Campbell brought a heavily built sorrel from the stables back of his rooming-house. He saddled it one-handedly and then vaulted on to the horse's back.

'Quick — git up in front of me!' he ordered, pointing the gun. Sylvia obeyed and his powerful arm tightened about her waist. Soon they were out in the main street and heading for the trail leading to Carl Naylor's ranch. Sylvia made no effort to break free of the gunman's grip. She was satisfied he would keep himself in check for fear of Naylor. She relaxed, fighting the desire for sleep.

In fifteen minutes they had reached the Leaning L. Campbell lifted Sylvia down from the saddle and marched her ahead of him to the big, wide porch. His hammerings on the locked screen-door eventually brought Naylor himself, hastily dressed in pants and shirt, a gun in his hand.

'What in blazes is the idea?' he demanded; then the moonlight revealed his change of expression as he caught sight of Sylvia standing there.

'I found this dame rootin' in your office, boss,' the gunman explained, with a definite note of pride in his voice. 'I figured you mightn't like it an' would want to question her — '

'You figured right,' Naylor said

grimly. 'Come inside, both of you.'

He led the way into the big, airy living-room and lighted the twin oil-lamps. His lips venomously tight, he turned to consider Sylvia with contemptuous eyes.

'My office, eh? How much good d'you think that would do you?'

'Plenty of good if this gorilla hadn't blasted his way in.'

Naylor grinned widely. 'You sure have a yen, Syl, for sticking your pretty nose into trouble. I've only to hand you over to the sheriff as a trespasser and he could yank you off to jail for one to five years. There's a witness to prove it, too — Rocky here. Altogether it's a pretty nice setup, isn't it?'

'I think,' Sylvia answered, her eyes glinting, 'that you don't hold all the aces this time, Carl! This is the man who kidnapped me,' Sylvia glanced towards Campbell. 'Once you hand me over to the sheriff I'll very soon tell him all the facts. I've no doubt he'll find some method by which to make this man talk!'

Scowling, Naylor contemplated his gun.

'You ain't got any proof that it was me — ' Campbell began, then Carl cut him short.

'Shut up, you damned fool! That in itself is as good as an admission. I guess the answer is that the girl's recognized your damned voice.'

'You bet I have!' Sylvia declared. 'Campbell here is living, breathing evidence that I was telling the truth when I said I was kidnapped. From that it's only a very short step to having the whole case of Neil re-tried — and you know it!'

'Yes, I know it,' Carl nodded slowly. 'And in a case like this the only method is to destroy the evidence! That's a sure-fire way of making certain nobody ever finds out anything!'

Rocky Campbell gave a start and his gun swung round. Before he could level it, however, Carl's Colt blazed relentlessly, three times. The gun-hawk stood for a moment, staring blankly, his own weapon tumbling out of his hand. Then his knees buckled and he collapsed on his face.

Carl looked down at him, the cordite fumes curling about his nostrils. His dark, piercing eyes fixed on Sylvia's aghast features.

'Any further notions about evidence?' he asked briefly.

'This is cold-blooded murder!' she whispered. 'Nothing else! I always knew you held life pretty cheaply, but *this* . . . ' She turned away, sickened.

'He was a murderer many times over,' Carl said. 'I guess he'd have gotten it in the end, one way or the other. Better now, before he could talk. Right now the only other ones who know anything are those who did the rustling — and they know better than to talk. You know plenty, of course, but without proof you're stymied.'

Sylvia said nothing. Carl caught her shoulder and swung her round roughly.

'I'm talking to you!' he shouted. At

that moment the door flew open and a heavy-set man came hurrying in, his gun at the ready.

As he saw the body on the floor, and then Carl and the girl standing beside it, he put his gun back in its holster and aimed an enquiring glance at Naylor.

'What happened, boss?' he asked. 'I heard the shots from over by the bunkhouse an' thought I'd better come an' see what was goin' on.'

'I guess Rocky spoke out of turn,' Carl said. 'Guess I don't like his body left cluttering up the place, either. Ditch it somewhere, quick!'

The man nodded, heaved the body on to his shoulder, and then went from the room. Carl turned back to Sylvia.

'My loyal foreman,' he explained, slipping his Colt back into its holster. 'And since he doesn't know a thing about my activities in framing Neil it won't do you any good.'

Sylvia sat down heavily, gripped by tiredness. She raised her eyes and looked at Naylor bitterly.

'There are going to be questions asked about Campbell. I should think he's well enough known around town for his sudden departure to be noticeable. When I tell the sheriff you shot him because he could have proved Neil's innocence, he'll listen, and — '

'There'd only be your word for it,' Carl interrupted. 'Just the same,' he continued, musing, 'there are three slugs from my gun buried in Rocky's body. If you talked, the sheriff might decide to look for the body and match up the slugs. That would be tough on me ... unless I had a reasonable excuse. And I think I have! In spite of all that's happened, Syl, I still aim to marry you! Mebbe that sounds crazy!'

'Crazy is right!'

'Is it? Supposing your promising to marry me got Neil and that Indian free? What then? I know you'd keep a promise. You're that kind of a girl.'

'I wouldn't marry you under any pretext whatever!' Sylvia snapped.

'I suppose,' Carl continued, now

talking half to himself, 'that I could dig those three slugs out of Rocky if need be — but if you talked to the sheriff and he was in the mood to believe you he'd reckon it *more* suspicious to find the bullets dug out rather than left in. Either way, he might look into things. Yeah, mebbe I was a bit hasty. But there's a neat way round it — using you and Neil both!'

'Neither of us would ever help you!'

'Hear me out first.' Carl smiled. 'If you'll promise to marry me I'll go to the sheriff before the hanging tomorrow and tell him that I caught Campbell snooping around my spread tonight, and shot him down as a trespasser. But before dying he admitted that he was behind all the rustlings and switched the blame to Neil because he was one of the poorest ranchers around here and needed to make money because of you coming. That'll do two things at once — clear Neil and put me straight. The law says you can shoot a trespasser on sight in these parts and you'll have to confirm that I shot him down in the midst of thieving, and threatening you. I reckon your word will add plenty of weight to things.'

'Never!' Sylvia retorted. 'You're not going to turn me into a liar just so as you can escape your just deserts. I mean to tell the sheriff the truth this very night — ' She broke off as Carl seized her shoulders and shook her violently.

'Get this through your head, Syl! I'm not letting you leave here tonight. You've only one chance of saving Neil's life, and that is to bear out my story. You verifying what I say will be enough. Neil will automatically be cleared . . . ' Seeing the girl's indecision, he added:

'You don't have to marry me till I've carried out my side of the bargain and gotten Neil released. If it goes wrong you're under no obligation, but if it goes right we'll be married pronto.'

Still Sylvia hesitated. 'You don't suppose Neil will let you get away with it, do you?' she demanded. 'He *knows* you framed him, and he'll never let you rest.'

'He only *thinks* it was me who framed him. He can't prove it — ever; and he sure won't do anything more once he's escaped the rope, because he'll be quite convinced you're on my side and not his. He'll hate you for that — and then act like you'd never even existed.'

'So that's it. I sell myself to you and condone cold-blooded murder in order to free him!' Sylvia clenched her fists and stared up into Carl's grimly smiling face.

'That's right. It all depends if you love him enough to do it.'

For several moments Sylvia was silent, then she gave a hopeless shrug.

'All right, it looks as though you have me checkmated. You have my promise to marry you, but only if you free Neil and Fleeting Cloud and save their lives. One slip-up in doing that and the deal's off.'

Carl gave a hard smile. 'I always did

think you were a girl with plenty of sense.'

Sylvia succeeded in getting little more than an hour's sleep in an armchair in the ranch-house living-room, before Carl's shaking of her shoulder aroused her.

'Time to be moving,' he told her, and she saw that he was fully dressed and ready for departure. 'I'll show you where you can freshen up — and I'm taking no chances on you getting away, so don't get any ideas.' Sylvia gave him a look of contempt and followed him from the living-room.

Ten minutes later they hit leather for Nathan's Cleft, Sylvia riding a swift pinto that Carl had provided for her. All the time they rode side by side he kept one hand on the butt of his Colt in case she attempted anything.

When they arrived in the town they found that despite the earliness of the hour preparations for the hanging party were already well advanced. The denizens of the town were lining the boardwalks or gathered in a big watching circle about the giant sycamore at the far end of the street, which on many other occasions had given its lowest branches in the cause of justice.

Carl drew his horse to a halt, Sylvia beside him, and they sat for a while watching the activity.

'Well, what are you waiting for?' Sylvia demanded, giving him a hard glance. 'The sheriff will be in his office. It's time you got busy.'

At that moment the sheriff appeared, together with two deputies and the mayor. In their midst, their hands secured behind them, came Neil and Fleeting Cloud. Neil paused for a moment as he saw the crowd, then his gaze strayed over to where Sylvia and Carl were seated on their horses.

To her dismay, Sylvia realized how things must look — just as if she and Carl were firm friends who had turned up to watch the grim proceedings. She tried by expressions to give Neil some sign of the real purpose in her being present, but she was too far away in the dim grey light. He turned away in apparent contempt and walked over to the sycamore tree.

'OK, this is where I go into action,' Carl said, and dismounted preparatory to pushing through the crowd. But before he could do so things began to happen.

From the direction of the trail along which he and Sylvia had travelled earlier there suddenly came the thunder of hoofs. Sylvia hipped round in the saddle and gazed in amazement on a party of some eight horsemen, masked with bandannas, firing their guns in the air and hurtling their mounts down on the gathered crowd. Instantly the people scattered for safety and Sylvia too swung her pinto to one side as the gunmen came thundering on.

They ploughed through the clear passage the spectators had made and went on their way towards the sycamore tree — then, in full view of everybody they swept up Neil and Fleeting Cloud before it could be fully grasped what was happening.

Immediately the sheriff and his deputies had their guns out and fired desperately after the retreating rescuers — but it was too late. The suddenness and perfect timing of their swoop had done the trick and they were already becoming remote as they hurtled down the opposite trail that led into the grey dawn.

'Horses — quick!' Sheriff Holton yelled, leathering his gun. 'Get after 'em!'

Sylvia's eyes glowed with delight. Neil had been rescued, and no doubt would take good care he stayed that way, at least until he could prove his innocence.

'Hell, that was quick,' Carl commented, in grudging admiration, emerging from the shouting throng. 'I don't think I — '

'And it lets me out with you, Carl!' Sylvia interrupted. 'You'll have to find yourself another wife — if you live that long!'

She whipped round her pinto and gave Carl's horse a crack across the withers, sending the animal scampering away in fright just as Carl was about to mount. That was all the head start Sylvia needed to get away.

Digging in her spurs she jolted the fast little pinto into action and swung round, leaving the town in the opposite direction to that which the rescuers had taken. The moment she gained the trail she bore right up the grassy-bank to the pastureland; then, taking in a wide detour, she moved in the direction of the horsemen, still faintly visible far away amidst plumes of dust as they headed towards the mountains.

Her teeth set, the wind flinging back her blonde hair, Sylvia rode hard, the little pinto's hoofs drumming incessantly on the earth as she tore onwards.

Neil, for his part, found his ropes slashed as the men who had snatched him kept up their terrific pace. Fleeting

Cloud was also released, riding double-saddle, as was Neil, with one of the rescuers.

'Thanks a lot, fellers,' Neil panted, as the horsemen pulled down their bandannas and revealed friendly, familiar faces. 'Who's behind this rescue?'

'Ma, of course,' answered the man with whom he was riding. 'She spent all last evenin' in the Lucky Chance arrangin' the set-up with us, timin' it exactly. She'd make a mighty good general! Right now she's waitin' for you at Calamity Mine.'

'She is, huh?' Neil grinned. 'Trust her to think of a place like that!'

Calamity Mine was an abandoned gold working, the cave-in of which had killed some two hundred miners many years before, hence its name. But as a hideout it could hardly be bettered, going deep into the earth, and with many of its tunnels dry and habitable.

Twenty minutes' hard riding and the journey was over as the sun came up. Neil found himself led through the salt-white dust of the mine area to the shaft props. Since there was no cage he had to climb down the hundred feet into an oil-lighted gloom. He had time to notice that there were bedrolls, ammunition cases, provisions, and other essentials — then Ma came hurrying out of the shadows to greet him.

'They got you!' she cried thankfully, hugging him tightly. 'I always knew I could count on them boys!'

'The wonder to me is that you weren't in on it yourself with that rifle of yours!' Neil laughed.

'That wouldn't have been smart, son. The boys rode masked so's nobody could know afterwards who they are. But I'd have been recognized pronto. Here, come an' sit ye down. There's a breakfast ready an' everything set. All this stuff was moved down here during the night in readiness . . . You'll want a meal too, Fleet,' she added, looking at the immobile Indian, and he promptly nodded.

Neil settled at the upturned crate that was doing duty as a table and tackled the meal awaiting him. Ma stood and considered him, then she glanced round as presently the rest of the boys came climbing down from the surface.

'How's about the horses, Ma?' Neil asked suddenly. 'When the sheriff starts searching in this direction he's liable to find them!'

'Don't fret yourself, son. I figured everythin' out. Them cayuses have a tunnel all their own. There's an old truck ramp leadin' to it, an' the entrance is easy to cover with rock. We're quite safe down here. Only wish there was some gold, too. Supposed to be some hereabouts but I ain't had the time to look. Mebbe I will afore I'm through. Gold'd come in mighty useful, since I'm not gittin' no younger!'

Neil smiled and reflected for a moment, then went on with his breakfast, Fleeting Cloud eating steadily beside him and swallowing the coffee

Ma provided at intervals from the portable oil-heater.

The rest of the men settled with their backs to the tunnel wall, and joined them in the meal. Ma surveyed them and then grinned.

'I want to thank you, boys, for what you did,' she said.

'Weren't nothin', Ma,' one of them answered. 'Neil's one of our pardners, ain't he? We all know that rustlin' sentence was a dirty frame-up.'

Neil, his hunger satisfied, rolled himself a cigarette.

'Sure, Carl Naylor framed me,' he agreed, his mouth setting. 'But I just can't stop down here and wait for a miracle. I've got to get some evidence out of him to show what he did to Fleet and me.'

'An' git yourself hogtied again?' Ma demanded. 'If there's any proof-gettin' to be done from that snake Naylor I'm the one who'll get it! The sheriff can't stop me neither since I'm in the clear . . .'

Ma began pacing, thinking furiously. 'Up to now,' she resumed, 'I've only concentrated on gittin' you both away from the rope. If any of the rest of you boys have any suggestions let's have 'em,' she invited.

There was silence for a time. 'I saw Syl and Naylor just before I was snatched free,' Neil said, lighting his cigarette. 'All spruced up she was, sitting on a pinto right beside him. I could forgive her plenty, but not her turning up purely to see me hang.'

'That gal never was any good!' Ma growled. 'Last night when I was in the Lucky Chance arrangin' for this rescue, she turned up, lookin' all charm an' polish, an' went straight to Naylor's private room. They was half an hour in there then she came dashin' out with him half-drunk shoutin' after her. Ain't no doubt in my mind from what he said that they'd bin havin' a nice time. Forgit her, son.'

'Hard job, forgetting her,' Neil muttered. 'I keep thinking there must be some kind of explanation for her siding with Carl the way she's doing.'

'If there is, she had a chance to spill it to me last night when she cleared her belongings out of the spread. But she didn't. She simply told me that I didn't seem much sorrow-stricken since I could drink beer in the saloon with you under sentence of death. Then she quit, bag and baggage apart from that trunk of hers which I dumped on the trail outside . . . ' Ma broke off and swung suddenly to her rifle.

The other men got on their feet too, guns out of their holsters. Fleeting Cloud drew his knife, his implacable eyes glancing from Ma to Neil.

'Somebody a-climbin' down the shaft,' Ma whispered at last, her face grim. 'Jason, stand by to hogtie him — but no shootin' . . . Rick, see who it is. Be one of the sheriff's boys, mebbe.'

Rick, keeping close to the tunnel wall, glided to the big circular opening that gave on to the old shaft. He peered outside as the sounds came nearer. As he did so there came a sudden cry from the intruder. A rung of the corroded old ladder snapped and Rick was just in time to see a dim figure come hurtling down. The figure struck the thin tunnel floor and disappeared clean through it.

'What in the hell's goin' on?' Ma's voice demanded, and Rick turned his weather-beaten face towards her.

'Durned if I rightly know, Ma. Somebody fell off the ladder when a rung broke. He's gone clean through the floor here!'

Ma swept up the oil-lamp and in a group, the rest of the men hurried to the hole where the intruder had crashed through. The rays of the lamp alit on a struggling figure below.

'For land's sakes, it's the gal!' Ma exclaimed, astonished.

Instantly Neil hurried forward, lying face down as he peered into the small cavern below.

'Hey there, Syl! You OK?' he cried.

'Bruised as hell,' she answered bluntly, looking up and feeling too knocked about to be refined. 'Get me out of this confounded place — '

'Say, wait a minute!' Ma interrupted, and Neil looked at her sharply. 'Just take a look at the wall behind the gal, son!'

Everyone looked, along with Sylvia herself. She was perhaps ten feet below in the little cavern — and behind her, and indeed all around her, the lamp-light was being reflected back from irregular gleaming veins in the rock.

'Sweet Hades, *gold*!' Neil yelped. 'A whole damned seam of the stuff! Gold!'

Her eyes glittering, Ma levered herself into the cavity and dropped at Sylvia's side, then took the oil-lamp Neil handed down to her before he came down himself. Sylvia, smudged and wincing, watched Ma as she inspected the rock carefully.

'No doubt about it!' she said at last. 'Sure is gold. This mine was abandoned out of respect for the dead before this seam were ever found, an' I guess the gal here hit straight on it.' She turned to look at Sylvia directly. 'Don't make much difference to what I think of you personally, gal, but you sure found somethin'. This lot's worth a mint! I'm stakin' a claim on it the moment I can.'

'You bet!' Neil agreed hurriedly. 'But in the meantime let's get Syl out of here. Up you get,' he added, and by main strength levered her up to the cavity opening, where Fleeting Cloud took charge and lifted her safely to the floor of the old tunnel.

In another moment she was in the main cavern, waiting in the dark. Ma, still flushed with the discovery of gold, came into view with the oil-lamp, then waddled across to the crate that was doing service as a table and set the lamp down.

'Mighty nice discovery,' she breathed, half to herself, and the men grouped around her looked at each other and nodded. Each one of them, proven and loyal, knew that they would share later in whatever Ma decided to do with her fortuitous gold strike.

'Not a word about this to anybody,' she said suddenly, her finger raised and her voice sharp. 'If news of this once gits out we'll not get a blasted nugget of it. That includes you, gal.'

'Of course,' Sylvia agreed, then she added, 'I'm — I'm glad I happened on it as I did. And I'm also glad that I managed to find you.'

'Not so sure I am — apart from the gold,' Ma told her sourly. 'Like as not Sheriff Holton has followed you — '

'Most unlikely, Ma. He hadn't started from town when I last saw him. I kept you in sight all the way here. The dust haze was sufficient guide for me.'

'Where's your hoss?' Ma snapped.

'Outside, at the shaft top.'

'Then you can git on it an' blow — mighty quick!'

'Give her a chance, Ma,' Neil implored. 'Jason, go and put her horse with the others so's it won't be a clean give-away.'

Jason went out and Sylvia looked hungrily down at the remains of the breakfast, together with the coffee, on top of the crate.

'Can I have some?' she asked quickly, and without waiting for an answer poured coffee into the tin cup Neil had been using. He watched her in aloof, troubled silence.

'What you playin' at, gal?' Ma demanded. 'Ain't you got the brains to know when you're not welcome?'

'I hardly expected you to greet me with open arms after seeing me with Carl Naylor so much,' Sylvia confessed, slapping butter on to a hunk of bread and eating it hungrily. 'But that was only the way things *seemed*. I *had* to go around with Carl in order to try and get something on him — so I could free you, Neil.'

'Why should you want to do that?' he asked curtly. 'You don't love me. You've never forgiven me for telling you I had a big ranch when I hadn't.'

'I can have a love of justice, can't I? I know as well as you do that Naylor framed you, so I acted the way I did to try and prove it.'

'And found out what?' Ma enquired bitterly.

'Plenty! I even got Carl to admit he framed Neil, but without any witnesses, it didn't do me much good.'

'You actually got that far?' Neil's eyes widened.

Sylvia related the details as she ate, including the incident of the shooting of Rocky Campbell. When she had finished Neil was looking at her with an eager light in his eyes, whilst his mother was dourly considering something for herself.

'Well, that puts everything right,' Neil exclaimed. 'You did everything you did just to wheedle the truth out of Naylor!'

'Uh-huh,' Sylvia agreed, shrugging. 'Thank heaven I didn't have to keep my promise to marry him. If it had come to that I'd have had to find some way to escape.'

'Why the heck didn't you tell me what you was doin'?' Ma demanded.

'I didn't say anything, Ma, because

201

you were so obviously determined to think other things about me. I thought it might help if you went on thinking them, then no information to the contrary could possibly have reached Carl and put him on his guard. The more I seemed to be for him the more he'd be likely to tell . . . '

Her voice trailed off as apparently a thought struck her. After a moment or two she sat down on the edge of the crate before putting it into words.

'The one chance we have left is to prove to the sheriff that Carl shot Rocky Campbell — and to explain that he shot him because he was dangerous evidence. Carl's afraid of that move.'

'Yeah,' Ma growled. 'An' the first thing he'll do will be to dig the slugs out of Campbell's carcass so's to destroy the evidence. Holton can think what he likes, but without them slugs he can't prove a thing.'

'True, but if he found the bullets had gone he might — as Carl himself suggested to me — consider it so suspicious as to look into things more carefully. No, I think he'll let sleeping dogs lie and hope that you — both of us in fact — won't be caught.'

'Else git rid of his gun,' Ma mused.

Neil shook his head. 'Too risky, Ma. That gun of his is a special job — walnut-butt and pearl inlay. If he ditched it some place everybody would notice it had gone. Figuring it all out,' he finished, musing, 'I guess he'll probably play possum for the moment and only act if he has to. His only worry is that Syl might tell the sheriff everything.'

'If we could find Campbell's body with the bullets in it — and also make that blacksmith talk somehow — we'd really be getting somewhere,' Sylvia said, thinking.

'Findin' Campbell's body won't be so easy,' Ma said.

'I don't think so!' Sylvia insisted. 'Carl told his foreman to get rid of it. All that has to be done is make the foreman talk. Threatening to put a bullet through him should do the trick,' she finished calmly.

'Durn it, gal, y'can hardly hold a gun yet, let alone throw a scare into a hard-baked foreman.'

'I was relying on you to do that,' Sylvia explained coolly, and Ma gave a start. 'It's perfectly obvious that Neil can't take any active part because the moment he is spotted he'll be recaptured and dealt with.'

'Yeah,' Ma agreed. 'But that doesn't stop the boys here from doin' somethin', does it?' The assembled men nodded promptly, then looked surprised as Sylvia shook her blonde head.

'If they don't return to their normal occupations in Nathan's Cleft the sheriff will know which men made that rescue and they'll be roped in as well. It isn't fair on them. Now they have done their rescue act they should be allowed to resume their ordinary occupations.'

'Syl's right,' Neil admitted. 'Provided Fleet and I are given revolvers we can easily look after ourselves, whoever comes. There's no use in you boys sticking your necks out any further.'

'So you're figurin', gal, that I'm goin' to tackle that foreman all on my own, huh?' Ma asked drily.

'Not at all. I'm coming with you.' Sylvia cast a defiant look about her. 'For one thing I want to get my own back on Carl: I want to find a means of proving what a crook and swine he really is. When it comes to gun-play I don't pretend to be so hot — though maybe I could manage at a pinch — but my main aim in trying to get evidence is to do the thing ourselves.'

'Then what's your plan?' Ma asked.

'Wait until it starts to get dark tonight, and Carl goes to his saloon. That will leave the way clear to get at that foreman of his. Once he has a gun on him he'll be more or less forced to obey. When we have that body — with the bullets still in it, I hope — we can take it into town and let the sheriff take a look at it. The rest will be up to him. He should move fast enough to check up on Carl's gun after the story I shall have to tell him.'

'Yeah, it might work, at that,' Ma assented. 'An' you're takin' all this risk, gal, just to try an' git your own back on Carl?'

'Partly, but also to prove Neil innocent. When we've done that, I'll feel satisfied. Perhaps I can even think about returning home.'

This brought silence for a moment. Neil looked at Sylvia steadily but did not say anything. Ma turned and contemplated the eight cow-punchers, who seemed to be wondering what to do.

'Leave three guns, boys, an' then be on your way,' she instructed. 'Better scatter as you leave. There's just a chance that the sheriff may be a-watchin' an' we don't want to give him any clues just yet. See you sometime later on when this mess has bin cleared up.'

The men nodded and left the tunnel together to return to the surface. Sylvia picked up one of the heavy .45 guns, which had been laid on the crate top.

'Know how to use it?' Ma enquired, with a cynical grin.

'I assume the principle is the same as a thirty-two I used to have,' Sylvia answered. 'A bit heavy, but I'll manage. I'm beginning to realize how true a statement you made about not getting far in this region without a gun.'

'That needn't worry you if you're intending to leave in the finish,' Neil remarked stiffly. 'Your brooch is undone, Syl. I'd better fix it.'

He reached out towards it and straightened the loose shaft as well as he could.

'This brooch is likely to get lost if you don't look out,' he said. 'Would you care very much if it did?'

Sylvia fingered it gently. 'I twisted it opening Naylor's office window,' she said. 'Certainly I don't want to lose it . . . it may come in useful.'

8

Holocaust

The pale, brief twilight had settled over the pastures of Nathan's Cleft. Lying on their faces amidst the sage were Sylvia and Ma Grantham, each with a .45 in hand, their heads slightly raised so that they could see the Leaning L ranch half a mile away in the gathered mists of the valley. Behind them, tethered to a giant cactus, were their two horses, hardly distinguishable from the monstrous growth itself.

Just at this point the terrain was mostly sand, stippled with clumps of sage. The only other signs of life lay in the occasional scuttling of a lizard, or a distant whirring from a sidewinder as they sensed the presence of humans.

The twilight deepened swiftly and the murderous heat of the day streamed out into the vacuum of space, being replaced by gathering, gripping cold.

Sylvia was grateful for the mackinaw Ma gave her from her saddle-bag.

'Thanks, Ma,' she murmured, as she buttoned it in place about her slim shoulders. 'Didn't think you cared about me.'

'Don't flatter yourself, gal. I just don't want you frozen stiff just when we need to git busy!'

Sylvia smiled at the unconvincing explanation.

'What's happened to the sheriff?' she asked. 'We saw no sign of him on our way here from Calamity Mine.'

'That critter'll be searchin' the one place where most outlaws and runaways got — the mountains. I'll gamble that Calamity Mine never entered his calculation. That's why I chose it.'

Both women became suddenly alert as they noticed a lone horseman set off and hit the trail leading to Nathan's Cleft.

'It's Naylor,' Ma breathed. 'Off to the

Lucky Chance for the night's business. I reckon that pretty soon his foreman will come out and start checkin' the corrals over for the night.'

She was right. A few minutes later he came into sight from the ranch bunkhouse and went across the yard to the inner gate of the corrals.

'Be too dark soon to see what he's doing,' Sylvia said, glancing at the darkening sky. 'What happens then?'

'The moment night falls we ride down there,' Ma responded. 'It'll take some time for him to finish his rounds.'

Night came with the abruptness of a drawn curtain. As if a switch had been thrown the stars glittered out of the vast upturned bowl of the sky. The night sounds became muted. The mist deepened, rolled, and spread like a swathe out of the depths of the valley.

'This mist is our chance.' Ma said, getting to her feet and shaking the sand impatiently from her clothes. 'It won't last long, but it's all we need. Come on. To the hosses.'

As they mounted in the starlight, Sylvia smiled momentarily at the odd figure the hard-bitten old girl cut. Her heavy check skirt had, due to her sitting astride her horse, dragged up to her knees. On her big feet were the inevitable elastic-sided boots with the thick soles, and Sylvia was surprised to notice a sheath knife jammed in the top of Ma's left boot, concealed on the inside of her leg and evidently for emergency use only.

'All set?' Ma enquired, cutting Sylvia's study short. 'Remember — if anythin' goes wrong, for God's sake, gal, try an' shoot first and ask all the questions afterwards!'

Sylvia nodded, her nerves tingling. She had spent most of the day in catching up on missing sleep, and now was ready for action. With Ma just ahead of her she cantered her pinto down the slope to the valley floor, and towards the dim outlines of the Leaning L ranch. In the murk ahead was the vague shape of a fence, from behind which came the rustling of beasts as they stirred in the big corrals.

'Hold it, gal.' Ma dragged her horse to a standstill. 'We can wait for him here. He has to pass us to git to the main gate of the second corral. When that happens we'll be ready for him.' She uncoiled a rope from the saddle horn and noosed it in readiness. Beside her Sylvia held her heavy .45 awkwardly.

'You can keep him covered, gal, whilst I rope him — that's the best way.' Ma pushed her own revolver into the belt about her skirt.

The mist was beginning to thin now that the cold of the night was becoming more equally distributed. Suddenly Ma whispered:

'Here he comes, gal! Keep that gun of yourn ready!' The foreman became visible, humming a tune to himself, moving along beside the fence.

'*Hold it!*' Sylvia snapped, pointing her gun.

Instantly the foreman swung round,

his hand dropping to his gun. Before he could grasp it Ma's well-aimed lariat descended over his shoulders, down to his wrists, and pinned his arms tight against his body. He swore luridly as he was dragged backwards and brought up with a thump against Ma's horse.

'Start walkin', feller!' Ma told him harshly. 'Once you're clear of this spread I'll tell you what you're goin' to do. Go on — walk!'

As the foreman hesitated, Ma spurred her horse suddenly, and since the rope was tied to the saddle horn the foreman had to go with it. Stumbling, tripping and cursing he ran along behind Ma's mount with Sylvia coming up in the rear, with the .45 still ready for action.

For several hundred yards Ma went on, then she drew to a halt, satisfied that the ranch was far enough away in the slowly dispersing mist.

'Now, feller,' she said ominously, looking down at the foreman's swarthy, baffled face in the starlight. 'You're agoin' to part with some information. If y'don't there's two forty-fives to take care of you.'

'Quit clownin' around, Ma!' the foreman panted. His tone belied the fact that deep down he was scared. He knew well enough the ruthless type of woman he was dealing with. 'What the hell can you want with me? I ain't done nothin'!'

'You've done plenty, feller — like buryin' Rocky Campbell's carcass for starters!'

'Ain't no crime to bury a dead body, is it?'

'I'm not a-goin' into that,' Ma retorted. 'Just show us where the body is, that's all. An' do it quick! I'm not sittin' here all blasted night.'

The foreman did not move. 'What in hell d'you want Campbell's body for?' he asked suspiciously. 'Since he's dead, it can't — ' He broke off as Ma yanked out her gun and pointed it at him steadily.

'Take us to where that body is, 'less

you fancy some lead poisonin'!'

That settled it. The foreman began moving, his arms still pinioned. Ma started her horse forward so that it kept pace with him. They kept going for nearly half an hour until they reached the edge of the desert.

The mist had vanished and the desert lay in limitless expanse under the cold, hard stars, the night wind sighing across it with a frigid breath.

'OK,' came Ma's voice. 'You don't get out of this noose, feller, 'til you show us where the body is.'

'Then how d'you expect me to dig it out?' the foreman demanded.

'Show us where it is first, then I'll figure out what has to be done.'

The foreman walked forward a few paces and stopped beside a scattering of feathery agaves.

'Right here,' he said. 'This plot of century plants is a sort of marker.'

'Keep me covered, gal,' Ma called up to Sylvia, sliding down from her horse. The noose suddenly lifted from the foreman and he flexed his arms. Ma snatched away his gun so that she now had one in each hand.

'Git busy!' she ordered. 'An' if you try any tricks God help you!'

The foreman went down on his knees and started burrowing in the sand. After a while, under his scraping hands, there began to appear the dark outlines of a body. And as this moment came the foreman suddenly acted with terrific speed.

Swinging round he flung a cloud of fine, biting sand into Ma's face. She spluttered and shut her smarting eyes. In that second she felt the guns whipped away from her hands.

'All right, both of you!' the foreman snapped, leaping to his feet. 'You up there on that cayuse — git down an' throw your gun over here right now!'

Sylvia tossed the gun over, then, swinging her leg over the saddle, she dropped to the sand. Ma stood blinking her eyes back into vision and regarding Sylvia angrily.

'Why the blue hell didn't you shoot, gal?' she asked bitterly. 'I told you to shoot at the first sign of trouble!'

'Sorry, Ma, I didn't fire because I was afraid I might hit you by mistake — you were right next to him, and . . . '

The foreman chuckled.

'Seems you didn't git yourself a very handy gunwoman, Ma! OK, now it's my turn with the questions: why the heck do you want Rocky Campbell's body?'

'You can go to hell,' Ma said bluntly. 'Ain't none of your business.'

'I reckon it is after you dragged me out here. I can think of only one reason: to see what sort of bullets there is in it an' then try an' match 'em up with the gun fired by the boss. I guess I'd sooner see him in the clear than at the mercy of any scheme a shrivelled wreck like you has thought up.'

Ma clenched her fists at the insult, but did not speak.

'I'll gamble that you wantin' this body has somethin' to do with Neil

Grantham's escape, 'bout which the boss is mighty sore,' the foreman continued. 'I guess y'know where he is and it'd help things a lot to git him back with the sheriff to finish the hangin' he should've got . . . '

'Just try it, you low-down skunk!' Ma breathed venomously.

The foreman sneered and fired one of the guns into the sand. The grains exploded over Ma's elastic-sided boots, but she remained stolidly unmoved.

'I ain't tellin' you or any guy else, not if you fire every blasted bullet into me,' Ma said defiantly.

'Mebbe the gal here will think different. She don't look the stubborn type. Hey — you there!' he shouted.

Sylvia came forward uncertainly in the gloom. Abruptly the foreman seized her left wrist and yanked her to him.

'Tell me where Neil Grantham is, or git a bullet where it can hurt plenty without killin' you!'

'Why not kill me and have done with it?' Sylia asked bitterly.

'Believe me, I'd like to do just that. I've no time for sassy dames like you — but it so happens I know that the boss has got certain notions about you bein' his exclusive property, and I daren't go quite that far. But I *can* still do this!'

Holstering his right-hand gun for a moment, the foreman lashed out his fist and struck Sylvia violently across the side of the jaw. She collapsed in the sand, her head spinning with agonizing pain.

'You dirty yellow hyena!' Ma shouted. 'I'll kill you for that — '

'Shut your trap, an' git wise to yourself, Ma!' the foreman blazed at her, twirling round. 'Ain't no reason why I shouldn't blot out a broken-down old has-been like you! But y'can save this gal gettin' knocked about plenty by telling me where your son is hidin'.'

'Don't tell him, Ma!' Sylvia implored, struggling to her feet and nursing her jaw. 'I don't care what he does to me . . . '

The fist lashed again and Sylvia saw something explode behind her eyes. Nearly stunned she dropped to her knees, a trickle of blood coming from her nostrils at the blinding blow she had received.

'Start talkin'!' The foreman gripped her upper arm and dragged her upwards. She reeled dizzily, still managing to gasp out a few words:

'I'm — I'm not telling a swine like you anything!'

The impact of his hand striking yet again sounded like a gunshot. Sylvia crashed flat on her back and hardly stirred. Ma quivered impotently as the gun still remained pointed towards her.

'So you're stubborn, just like this old bitch you go around with! But mebbe there's a way yet!' the foreman snarled, glaring down at the unmoving girl.

He drew back his heavy boot to deliver a smashing kick in her side — but before he could complete his sadistic performance something resembling a shadow flashed out of the silence and closed with him.

He gasped hoarsely as a sinewy forearm hooked under his chin and dragged him backwards, a hand gripping his gun-wrist at the same time. He tried to fire but the fingers of his attacker tightened inexorably, dragging upwards at the same time.

The foreman screamed as, with an excruciating wrench, his wrist-bone snapped and the revolver dropped into the sand.

'Fleet!' Ma yelled with delighted relief. 'Give the yellerbelly what's a-comin' to him! An' speed it up!'

The foreman fought and lashed frantically, but with remorseless strength the Indian forced him down into the sand and pinned him there, his fingers tightening into his windpipe.

The foreman bent his legs sharply and thrust upwards with his feet, striking the Indian savagely in the stomach. Fleeting Cloud gulped and relaxed for a moment — but only for a moment. As the foreman heaved himself up the Indian's murderous knife flashed three times in the starlight. A choked, gurgling gasp came from the foreman. He staggered, pitched sideways, then fell heavily and remained still.

Breathing hard, Fleeting Cloud wiped the knife on the body and returned his weapon to its sheath. He went over to where Sylvia was struggling up. He raised her gently and she passed the back of her hand over her blood-smeared mouth.

'Th-thanks, Fleet,' she whispered. 'I'll think a good deal differently about you in future.' The Indian held her slender, trembling body for awhile until she became a little steadier.

'What kind of miracle brought you breezin' in, Fleet?' Ma demanded. 'Did you follow us?'

The Indian nodded, his high-cheek-boned face expressionless in the starlight.

'I get it,' Ma growled. 'You thought a couple of mere women couldn't do the thing right? Or mebbe it was Neil's idea?'

Again Fleeting Cloud nodded and Ma gave a grunt.

'Guess you weren't far wrong, neither! It was a nice bit of shadowin', Fleet. We never saw you — but I guess we don't need you any more. With this jigger out of the runnin' we can finish the job for ourselves. Better go back and keep Neil company in case he gits in a spot while you're away.'

The Indian nodded and turned. Moving as soundlessly as ever he went to a shadowy darkness that was evidently his horse, mounted it, and was gradually enveloped in the night.

Ma came back from an examination of the foreman's body to where Sylvia was standing dabbing at her mouth with her handkerchief.

'He's dead,' Ma announced briefly. For a moment her hardness broke down. 'Hurt bad, gal?' she questioned, gripping Sylvia's shoulder and looking at her intently.

'Nothing I can't survive, Ma.' Sylvia tried to smile through her battered lips. 'No worse than a rough visit to the dentist.'

'I guess you've more courage than I ever figured,' Ma mused. 'For all you knew that hyena might've killed you by inches, but you still didn't tell him anythin'. Does me good to see it. Got plenty of tar in you after all.'

'Maybe,' Sylvia agreed. 'I reckon that deep down I might be a lot tougher than you've figured, Ma.'

'Huh?' Ma demanded. 'Do you know how you said that? Just like we talk around here.'

'Well, I've absorbed everything else from strong liquor, tough men, and blows in the face, so I might just as well make my language match as well!'

'Good gal!' Ma breathed, patting Sylvia's shoulder in delight. 'Now if you could only shoot like you can keep your trap shut under punishment . . . OK,' she added, moving, 'let's git to work, if you can stand it. We want Rocky

Campbell's carcass out of the sand and this foreman's in it instead. Then we're a-ridin' into town to look for Sheriff Holton.'

★　★　★

Carl Naylor was playing poker with one of his gunhawks in a corner of the Lucky Chance when a puncher came hurrying up towards him through the smoke-clogged room.

'Beat it,' Carl snapped, looking up from his cards as the man approached. 'I'm playing — come back later.'

'This won't wait,' the puncher insisted. 'Ma Grantham and the gal rode into town about ten minutes ago. I thought you might like t'know that Ma's got Rocky Campbell's body over her cayuse.'

Carl put down his cards, a hard light coming into his eyes as he stared up at the puncher. The man hurried on:

'Take a look-see for yourself if you don't believe me. I don't know if it means anything to you that Ma's gotten Rocky's body, but it might. Matter of fact, I've been wonderin' all day where that jigger had gotten to.'

'You talk too much,' Carl said curtly; then he got up and strode through the saloon, now nearly at the close of its evening's business.

He went out on to the boardwalk and stood gazing down the street in the direction of the sheriff's office. Two horses were at the hitch rail outside it. One of the animals had something dark slumped over the front of the saddle.

'See 'em?' The puncher had followed Carl through the batwings.

'I can see the horses and one of 'em carrying something — but I can't see Ma or the gal.'

'It was them all right, boss. They didn't see me. They was hammerin' on the sheriff's office door; but I guess he's still out with a posse lookin' for Neil Grantham.'

'So they must be sticking around there some place waiting for him, huh?

Mebbe that's just the way I like it.'

'Yeah? Meanin' what, boss?'

'Look, Shorty, the sheriff mustn't see that body of Rocky's. It might put me in bad, and the rest of the boys in with me. We've got to put Ma and that gal out of the way before Holton gets back — and ditch Rocky's body somewhere, too.'

The puncher waited as Carl thought the business out.

Then: 'Step on it and get the boys together. Six of 'em will do. I'll wait here.'

'OK, boss!'

Shorty fled back through the batwings; Carl remained where he was, his tall, powerful figure half-concealed by the boardwalk pillars. As he waited he saw signs of movement in the distance as Ma and Sylvia came slowly down the steps from the boardwalk outside Holton's office and then stood by their horses, apparently engaged in conversation. Naylor went into action.

His Colt leapt into his thinly

bandaged hand and he glided along the boardwalk, keeping well within the shadows. When he had come nearly opposite the two women he revealed himself suddenly, his gun levelled over the boardwalk rail.

'Evening, ladies,' he greeted drily, and Sylvia and Ma swung round, startled. 'Get your hands up!'

The two women exchanged looks and then slowly obeyed. Carl came down the steps to them, took their guns and stuffed them in his belt.

'Just like a coyote like you to sneak up on us without a sound,' Ma commented sourly.

'Yeah, isn't it?' Carl grinned slightly. 'I've a pretty good notion why you dug that body up! How'd you find it? Force my foreman to show you where he'd planted it?'

'We didn't use a divining rod, anyway!' Sylvia said.

Carl looked at her coldly, then he glanced up as the six men he had asked for came hurrying down the street.

'All of you fetch your horses!' he called. 'And hurry it up.' As the men turned away to follow the order, Carl resumed his study of Sylvia.

'You rode out on me pretty fast this morning when Neil was snatched. I've had time to think a good deal since then. Even if I did marry you I wouldn't ever be able to rely on you properly to keep quiet — so I've decided to ditch the idea of marrying you.'

'You've got one thing right, anyway,' Sylvia commented, smiling cynically.

'I'm going to wipe that smile off your face right now!' Carl snapped. 'I'm going to make it so that you can never open your mouth too wide. And you too, Ma!'

'Far as the gal's concerned she'd be better off dead than runnin' double-harness with a rat like you. What you got in that twisted mind of yourn?'

'For one thing, I've decided to blot out you and Sylvia — and I want your deaths to look like an accident so no blame can backfire on to me. For another, I want Rocky Campbell's body completely destroyed so it can't entangle me at any time in the future.'

'You always was one to make yourself safe,' Ma observed, and she spat hard at Carl's feet.

'After that, it'll simply be a matter of finding Neil and having him hanged, as it should have been at first — along with that slimy Indian, of course. Naturally, I don't suppose either of you will tell me where he is?'

'You'll git nothin' out of either of us. That right, gal?'

Sylvia nodded, tight-lipped.

'I expected that.' Carl shrugged. 'So I shan't waste any time.' He gave a cold smile. 'Remember that gorge Loco Lannigan threw himself into some time back, Ma?'

'Ain't nobody around here who don't. What about it?'

'You're going into the gorge as well — and Sylvia with you! A nice, carefully planned accident. One slip on the narrow trail past that shack where Loco used to live and you'll be finished! No mistakes — just a plain disappearance with death as the answer. As for Campbell, well I guess I can burn up his corpse in that shack of Lannigan's. It's been an eyesore for long enough.'

Carl said no more as his six henchmen came riding up in readiness, leading with them his own sorrel. Sylvia gave Ma a grim look, remembering the story of the madman who had shut himself up in that lone shack and shot at everybody within range until he had committed suicide.

'OK, ladies, on your horses,' Carl ordered, levelling his gun. Ma and Sylvia obeyed. Carl swung up into the saddle of his horse and led the way up the street, as the gunmen formed a tight circle about them.

Their hopes that they might run into the sheriff were not realized. The long journey to the lower mountain reaches ended when the arroyo that led to the foothills had been traversed and Carl called a halt on the narrow mountain trail.

'First we want to polish off this body of Rocky Campbell's — and for that we need that shack.' Carl nodded to where it stood a few yards away along the trail.

He rode his horse to it and then dismounted, his cohorts doing likewise. Ma and Sylvia remained in their saddles, powerless to do anything except watch.

'Put the body in the shack and then set the place afire,' Carl ordered; then he came back to where the women were waiting.

Ma eyed him. 'I'll bet there's only one thing worryin' you right now, Carl Naylor, an' that is that there body ain't alive so you could see it squirm.'

'I'm not a sadist,' Carl responded. 'Just practical — and able to take care of myself.' He looked at the women intently, then added:

'This trail goes about ten yards beyond the shack and ends in a direct drop into the gorge. Once your two horses are beyond the shack the fire will stop 'em coming back. The horses will be leery of it, see?'

'I'm beginning to get the picture,' Ma snapped.

'I want you to appreciate the full picture,' Carl said deliberately. 'The horses will plunge around plenty and finally fall into the gorge to escape the flames. The fire won't stay confined to the shack. It'll seize on the bushes at each side of the trail here. Roped to your saddles, you'll have no chance at all! Long before the sheriff can find you I'll have had one of the boys over to take the ropes away — otherwise it sure wouldn't look like an accident. Savvy?'

'Even if a snake were intelligent, it couldn't think of the things you do,' Ma commented. 'I reckon a snake's clean beside your sort.'

Carl took the lariat from the saddle horn of Ma's horse, and then tied her feet securely by fastening the rope under the animal's belly, bringing the rope up again so that Ma's wrists were securely bound behind her.

Using the lariat from his own horse he did the same to Sylvia, glancing around as the first soaring of sparks came from the shack. Immediately the man responsible came hurrying along the narrow trail.

'Right, on your horses,' Carl ordered, vaulting up to his own saddle. 'This needs nice timing. You fixed Campbell's body up OK?'

'Yeah,' Shorty answered. 'Right on top of the table in the livin'-room. He ought to go up like a blasted gorse bush in a forest fire.'

Carl nodded, his eyes fixed on the crackling flames. Their brilliance began to light the trail, their sparks drifted and smouldered in the bushes. Being tinder-dry the vegetation presently burst into flame.

'On your way, you two!' Carl slapped savagely at the withers of Ma's horse and Sylvia's. The two animals, already shifting uneasily, were stung into bounding forward, passing through the as yet clear gap between burning bushes and blazing shack. Not ten seconds after they had gone the flames leapt into each other and made a barrier.

'Timed it just about right.' Carl commented, glancing at his cohorts. 'We'd best stick around for a bit and see what happens. Them two might try and ride through somehow to get back. If they do that we'll settle 'em.'

'Are you quite sure they'll fall into the gorge, boss?' Shorty asked doubtfully.

'Course I'm sure, you bonehead! The horses are bound to panic as those flames spread along the bushes to the trail's end. They'll go over, sure enough. If we find they haven't we'll make 'em! In the meantime we're making 'em sweat plenty for the trouble they've caused us.'

Carl paused and continued to watch the now sizzling, raging flames intently. The walls of the shack had caught alight now and the interior was becoming visible through the roaring fire devouring the dust-dry logs.

Sylvia and Ma, on their pitching horses, were also watching the fire with an anguished intentness. They still had not gone over the trail edge, but it was looming dangerously close. In the other direction was the roaring barrier of flames and fast-burning bushes.

'Steady, boy, steady,' Ma ordered, as her horse lunged wildly. Then, as the animal's pitching brought her close to Sylvia:

'Hey, gal! We've still got one chance — and it's up to you!'

'What?' Sylvia panted. 'I'll try anything, Ma!'

'There's a knife in the top of my left boot. If you can git at it somehow an' put it in my hands I can durned soon work it across my ropes . . .'

The horses swung crazily away as Ma finished speaking and for one ghastly moment Sylvia thought they were going to plunge over the rimrock. They slid to a standstill, whinnied, then swayed round again in a panic-stricken circle, the whites of their eyes gleaming as they beheld the raging fire.

'I'll try, Ma,' Sylvia shouted, above the crackle of the holocaust. 'Try and keep your horse steady . . . I'll have to use my teeth.'

The horses whirled again. As Ma's left leg came near her, Sylvia swung down from the waist, her legs held firmly in the saddle by the rope under the horse's belly. Leaning as far sideways as she could she closed her teeth an inch from Ma's leg — then the horses suddenly whipped apart again.

It seemed an interminable time before they once more came side by side. Again Sylvia swung down, her body nearly horizontal to her horse and her teeth snapping frantically within an inch of the knife. A sudden lunge of her horse brought her head in collision with Ma's leg. Her teeth closed round the knife hilt and dragged fiercely upon it. She swung herself upright again, panting for breath.

'Give it to me!' Ma yelled. 'Git it into

my hands quick! These cayuses are loco with fright!'

Seizing her chance, Sylvia leaned over and rested her shoulder on the haunches of Ma's horse, releasing the knife from her teeth so that it fell across Ma's bound hands. Immediately Ma's fingers closed around the hilt and she worked the blade savagely up and down at an angle.

Suddenly it seemed that all hell had been let loose. A volley of explosions came from the roaring flames — shot after shot with the insistency and violence of a machine-gun. Bullets whined dangerously through the air, adding to the panic of the horses.

'That durned ammo Loco Lannigan used to have hidden!' Ma yelled, tearing her arms free. 'It's blowin' up!'

She unfastened her feet and jumped to the ground, freed Sylvia in a few seconds and she half-fell out of the saddle. Beyond the flaming screen Carl Naylor and his men were being carried helplessly away down the mountain trail, their horses panicked by the din of the explosions as well as the raging flames.

'We've got to try an' git Campbell's body out of that inferno somehow.' Ma said grimly, perspiration pouring down her face from the insufferable heat. 'It's our last bit of evidence . . . '

'OK, Ma, we might as well try and finish the job.' Sylvia dodged the lunges of the two horses. 'In any case we have to get through these flames to reach the trail again, haven't we?'

'Nope. We can do that easy enough when the fire's burned down. It won't git any fiercer than it is right now — but we've got to try an' git that body. Come on!'

9

Straight to the Heart

Neil, his back to the wall of the cavern, was gently dozing. Then he became suddenly alert as he saw Fleeting Cloud, sprawled beside him, sit up in the lamplight and listen.

The Indian moved silently to the mouth of the cavern and stood poised to detect distant sounds. Dimly, Neil heard them too now — the noise of what sounded like a savage gun-duel far away.

'What gives, Fleet?' he demanded, jumping up. 'Sounds like a gunfight!'

The Indian nodded and pointed upwards to indicate that they should leave their hiding-place. Quickly they mounted the crumbling ladder at the side of the shaft and presently scrambled over the rim, looking about them quickly in the starlight.

Far away — three miles at least — was the dancing red glow of a fire low down on the solid black bulk of the crouching mountains. From that direction too was coming the sound of revolver shots, carrying clearly on the still night air.

'I don't like it, Fleet,' Neil said. 'That sort of shooting could only be connected with either Naylor, Ma, or Syl. I guess it was a mistake ever to have left 'em to fend for themselves. Not with Naylor around.' The Indian gazed silently towards the distant fire and waited.

'We've got to get over there,' Neil decided. 'I'll have to take the risk of being caught. Get the horses out.'

Fleeting Cloud vanished like a wraith in the darkness. Neil gripped the handle of his holstered .45 and waited impatiently until the Indian, already mounted, came riding up with a horse alongside.

Neil swung into the saddle and both

men spurred their mounts at a killing pace through the sand and scrub which rolled away in the direction of the mountains' towering bulk. As they rode they saw the fury of the distant fire subsiding, but the light remained bright enough for them to use it as a guide. At length they came within measurable distance of the inferno.

'Unless I'm crazy, Fleet, it's old Loco Lannigan's place in the foothills,' Neil frowned. 'Though just why that isolated old dump should go up in smoke has me licked.'

He goaded his snorting, sweating horse on again up the arroyo that led to the foothills trail, the Indian coming up behind him. By the time they had reached the summit of the long acclivity the fire had died out to drifting sparks on the breeze.

Neil jumped from his horse, and with revolver in hand ran swiftly along the narrow mountain path, stopping as he came to the charred wood and smoking embers which had been the mad hermit's hideout. He looked about him at incinerated bushes and churned-up earth.

'No sign of anybody — yet we heard plenty of firing going on around here!' Neil holstered his gun as Fleeting Cloud joined him. 'I don't get it.'

The Indian, far more adept at reading signs in the ground than Neil, prowled about. But even he could make little of the churned-up earth, for having reached the end of the trail which looked down into the gorge he returned slowly and, dropping on one knee, moved the smoking ashes over with a piece of stick. Neil watched him for a while and then turned to begin an investigation on his own.

'Looks as if plenty of horses have been along here,' he said at length. 'Judging from these tracks it looks as if they travelled at high speed, in a panic to get away from the fire, mebbe . . . ' He broke off as the Indian nudged him, holding something in his palm.

Neil took the smoke-blackened object

and peered at it. The movement of his fingers upon it brought forth a bright gleam.

'Gold,' he muttered. 'Been warped by fire and — *My God, it's Syl's brooch!*' He gasped in alarm, and met the Indian's inscrutable eyes.

Fleeting Cloud pointed back to the embers to indicate where he had found the brooch, then he stood waiting impassively, as Neil stood thinking, turning the brooch over in his fingers.

'It looks as if Syl — and Ma too mebbe — got themselves mixed up in a fire and shooting affray. And if they were in *that* fire . . . ' He stopped, his voice breaking as he stared at the smouldering ruins of the shack.

The Indian, sensing what was coming, eased his deadly knife from its sheath.

'Only one man can explain this, Fleet,' Neil added grimly. 'Naylor! He'll likely be at his ranch this time of night so we're going straight after him right now!'

He swung round and hurried back in the direction of the horses. Then his hand flew to his holster as the rocks at the side of the trail suddenly sprouted men.

'Don't draw, Neil!' a heavy voice warned him. 'You're covered from every side.'

Neil waited, breathing hard. The men resolved into a party of perhaps ten. From their midst came the big figure of Sheriff Holton.

'I've finally caught up on you, Neil,' he announced, his voice hard. Then he took Neil's weapon and afterwards the Indian's.

'OK, so you've recaptured me,' Neil snapped. 'But for God's sake, Sheriff, let me get some unfinished business completed first. I was on my way to find Naylor. It's likely that he's murdered Syl and Ma — burned 'em to death back in the shack there.'

'Yeah?' In the starlight Holton glanced towards the smouldering embers. 'What was all the shootin' about? We heard it whilst we were out proddin' in the mountains for you — and saw the fire too. That's what brought us here.'

'Mv guess is that Ma and Syl put up a fight for it and that Naylor and his boys fired back. I don't know the facts yet, but I'll damned well find out! See this?'

'Well, what about it?' Holton said, peering at the warped brooch in Neil's hand.

'It belonged to Sylvia. It was loose, and I warned her that she was likely to lose it one day. Fleeting Cloud found it in these ashes, so I guess it sort of adds up, doesn't it?'

'Mebbe,' Holton said gruffly. 'But it seem to me that if anybody put paid to that gal it might be you — '

'What! Why, of all the damned — '

'I don't know 'bout your ma. I guess you wouldn't harm your own flesh an' blood, but it'd be different with the gal though.'

'For God's sake, man!' Neil stared in

amazement. 'That girl meant more to me than anybody else in the world! You don't suppose I'd kill her, do you? I loved her!'

'Like Hades you did!' Holton snapped. 'I don't forget the way you looked at her just before you were snatched from the hangin' party. If ever there was murder in a man's eyes it was in yours right then, when you looked at her on her horse sittin' beside Carl Naylor.'

'A hell of a lot has happened since then,' Neil argued. 'She followed me to the hideout afterwards and explained everything. I'd got the completely wrong impression. She was trying to get me free by working alongside Carl Naylor in the hopes he'd slip up and reveal something.'

'There's only your word for that,' the sheriff growled 'And I don't aim to stand here talkin'. I'm runnin' you in, Neil, along with Fleeting Cloud — and later on that sentence you escaped will be carried out. As to the girl and your ma, I'll make enquiries and find out what really happened to 'em. Even if I have got my own ideas about it.'

'All that you'll do is fall for whatever trumped-up line Naylor hands you,' Neil said bitterly. 'Because I'm convicted of a crime I never committed you'll believe him rather than me.'

'I know how to look after my own business, Neil. Right now we're ridin' back into town. And I'll take that brooch.'

Neil hesitated, then shrugged, his mouth set hard. The guns trained on him, he returned to his horse and mounted it, Fleeting Cloud doing likewise with his own animal. In silence they set off on the ride back along the narrow trail, the sheriff and his men coming up behind.

In half an hour they had reached the completely deserted town of Nathan's Cleft. In another ten minutes Neil and the Indian were in their separate cells at the back of the sheriff's little office.

'Wait a minute, Sheriff!' Neil implored,

as the key turned in the lock of the cell door.

'Well?' Holton waited, gazing between the bars in the dim lamplight.

'Before all this happened, you used to be one of my best friends. Surely that counts for something? The whole essence of the law is that a man should have every opportunity to prove that he's innocent.'

'Well, so what?' Holton waited, but his big face was still quite uncompromising.

'I *know* Carl Naylor framed me,' Neil stated deliberately. 'You can tail around with me, and with your boys too — out of sight, of course, but near enough to plug me if I try anythin'. Isn't that guarantee enough for you? If my efforts don't bring in the evidence you want you can do as you like with me. Either way I can't escape again. I've just got to find out what happened to Ma and Syl.'

For a long time the sheriff was plunged into deep thought, rubbing his square, bristly chin. Then at last he made up his mind and unfastened the door again.

'OK,' he said. 'But I'm not grantin' you a gun. A man with a gun has a chance of gettin' away and I'm not takin' the risk. You'll have to get along as best you can without it. And you're goin' to work alone,' Holton added. 'The redskin stays right where he is. Letting you out is risky enough without adding that slippery guy.'

'That's fine with me, Sheriff. Just let me out of here, that's all. First, I want a word with that blacksmith.'

Neil went ahead of the sheriff through the office. Together, he and Holton crossed the empty street and walked the few yards to where the blacksmith lived in a porticoed wooden shack beside his barred and shuttered forge.

Neil thumped heavily on the shack door. Holton drew back so that he was crouched on a level with the board-walk, his gun ready for any trickery that might ensue. Eventually the door opened and the massive figure of the blacksmith appeared. He was poking his shirt into the top of his pants as he peered out into the night.

'What in tarnation's the idea?' he demanded peevishly. 'I'm closed for the night.'

'This is a different kind of business,' Neil said, prodding his first two fingers into the small of the man's back. 'Outside! I want a few words with you, Ben.'

The blacksmith gave a start. 'Neil Grantham! What in hell — '

'I said outside!' Neil snapped. 'And make it quick!'

The blacksmith shuffled forward, his arms raised. At the rail of the porch he stopped.

'Don't turn around unless you want blasting,' Neil warned him. 'Now, start answering my questions. Not long ago you made a horseshoe specially to a cast given you by Carl Naylor, didn't you?'

'You're loco! I never did any such thing — '

'Listen, Ben, get this through your skull. My life depends on getting a straight answer out of you, and I don't care how far I go. I'll kill you to get at the truth if I have to. You *did* make a shoe for Naylor, didn't you? He bribed you to keep your mouth shut, didn't he?'

'No!' the blacksmith retorted stubbornly.

'If that's the way you want it, feller,' Neil breathed, 'start moving to your forge. When we're there we can get the fire started up.'

'What in hell for?'

'There's an old custom around here. Sometimes a traitor who can save a man's life and doesn't gets a brand on his forehead — a big 'T' seared in with a red-hot iron . . . And that's what *you* are going to get!'

The blacksmith shifted uneasily but said nothing. Neil went on remorselessly:

'When everybody in town starts talking and asking what the brand's for you're going to feel mighty uncomfortable. You'll have to quit town, hit the trail, and become an outcast or outlaw if you're to live at all. And don't think I wouldn't do it, neither! It's likely your actions led indirectly to the death of my mother and the girl I loved. I've sure as hell no liking for you, feller! Now get moving.'

The blacksmith made a half-turn and then swung round. Fully prepared for it, Neil clenched his fist and slammed it with shattering force into Ben's face. Ben keeled backwards with a throaty gasp, smashed through the portico rail, and collapsed in the dust of the street. Neil leapt on top of him, seizing his powerful arms in an immovable lock and dragging the blacksmith to his feet.

'We'll finish the job at your forge,' Neil panted, his free hand jabbing revolver-wise into the man's back.

'Wait!' Ben gasped hoarsely. 'I don't

see why I should get branded just to keep Carl Naylor sittin' pretty . . . Yeah — I *did* make a shoe from a cast he brought me.'

'OK,' Sheriff Holton said, stepping out of the shadows with his gun levelled. 'That's all I want to know, Ben. You're comin' with me to keep a cell warm, charged with perjured testimony. Start movin' across the street. Nice work, Neil,' he added.

Bewildered, but forced to obey, the blacksmith lumbered across the street and finished up inside the cell that Neil had formerly occupied. As he and the sheriff came out into the night again Neil said:

'Do you believe me now, Sheriff?'

'I'm beginnin' to,' Holton admitted. 'Just the same, I think you'd better finish what you've started before I think of puttin' my hardware away. Who comes next on your list? Carl Naylor?'

'You bet!' Neil retorted. 'He'll be at his spread this time of night. Let's be going.'

He mounted his horse, still outside the sheriff's office, and Holton swung up to his own mare beside him. Side by side they rode hard and fast through the cold night air, across the pasture-lands, until the Leaning L loomed up in the distance.

'As before, I'll keep out of sight, but where I can watch and listen to what happens,' Holton said, when they had gained the ranch yard. 'The rest's up to you, feller.'

Neil dismounted and strode up the three steps to the porch. He knocked heavily and then moved to one side, waiting. There was a long pause and the screen door swung.

He remained motionless in the deep shadow, waiting. After a moment or two Carl Naylor came out on to the porch, dressed in shirt and trousers. His gun gleamed in his hand as he looked around him.

Then Neil sprang, his fingers closing round Carl's gun-wrist at the same moment. A sharp twist and the gun went clattering away along the porch floor.

Unaware of the identity of his attacker, Carl fought back immediately, bringing up his free left fist with a killing blow to Neil's jaw. Neil jolted under it, and fell back hard against the wall. His vision blurred, he had time to see Carl hurtling towards him. Instinctively he brought up his knee and jammed it in the saloon-owner's stomach, stopping his onrush amidst an explosion of breath.

Using the wall to spring himself forward, Neil swung up a short-armed jab that took Carl under the chin. Carl crashed backwards into the dark hall of his ranch, got up, and received another hammer blow that sent him spinning helplessly into the living-room where one of the twin oil-lamps glowed brightly on the table. Evidently he had lighted them before answering the door.

At the table Neil stopped, his fists clenched, his chest heaving. Slowly Carl got to his feet, his eyes glaring.

'What in blue hell's the idea?' he demanded savagely.

'Y'know damned well what the idea is!' Neil retorted. 'After what you did to Ma and Syl, I've barely started on you yet.'

'Ma and Syl?' Carl repeated, staring. 'I haven't done nothing to 'em.'

'Quit lying! From the look of things Syl at least died in that madman's hut up on the rimrock. And you're the man who can explain that fire there, along with plenty of other things, if anybody can. You'd better start explaining it right now!'

'I tell you I don't know anything about Ma and Syl,' Carl yelled. 'Sure that shack burned down, but far as I know they weren't in it.'

'Then where are they? Where did they go?'

'I don't know — or care, either.'

'You'd better tell me, Carl, or I'll beat the truth out of you. What was all the shooting back on the rimrock about?'

'Some ammo hidden in the shack by that lunatic Lannigan went up in the flames, that's all. Scared the living daylights out of the horses.'

Neil strode forward purposefully, and Carl clenched his fists in readiness.

'I know Syl and Ma got as far as finding the body of Rocky Campbell,' Neil said deliberately, 'but after that something happened and that's where you come in. Spit it out, Carl, or I'll beat the tar out of you.'

Carl's response was to lash up a left uppercut with lightning speed.

Neil jerked his head sideways and swung round a terrific blow with his right. It missed and he went stumbling forward. In the split second's advantage Carl whirled up a heavy chair over his head and swung it down savagely towards Neil. Neil dodged the main impact but the blow struck his shoulder, numbing it for a moment. A punch in the jaw immediately afterwards spun him round and he crashed over on to the floor.

Instantly Carl dived for him, and after a further brief struggle, before Neil could fully recover, he found himself pinned down in a vicious armlock.

'Wriggle all the hell you like,' Carl said sourly. 'You'll never break this hold no matter how hard you try. Up you get!'

Both his arms in the wrenching grip behind him, Neil had to obey. He was bundled across the room to where long crossed knives hung X-fashion on the log wall. Carl grinned as he took one of them down with his free hand.

'I aim to kill you — as an intruder and a wanted man!'

Neil struggled impotently but the tension of Carl's one-handed hold was excruciating under the least movement. Panting hard, Neil stared at the gleaming blade in the saloon-owner's left hand.

Neil's arms were pinned but his legs were not. So as the blade whirled in a murderous arc he kicked his heavy riding-boot with all his strength, delivering a savage blow on Carl's shin. With a yell of anguish Carl momentarily released his hold and the swing of the knife petered out.

Round came Neil's fist with pile-driver effect, striking Carl full in the face. Carl tumbled back, clutching for the table — and missed it. His heels caught in the skin rug and at last he crashed half-senseless into the fire grate. Piled-up logs rolled in all directions, some falling on top of him.

In one bound Neil was astride him, the point of the knife just touching Carl's throat exactly at the jugular, close enough for him to feel the deadly cold of that murderous, needle-pointed tip.

'I want the facts, Carl,' Neil breathed. 'I'm already on the run from a rope, so I won't hesitate over slitting your throat if you don't talk! Now, what happened to Syl and Ma?'

'Blast you, *I don't know!*' Carl shouted, desisting in his struggling as the point of the knife became a trifle more emphatic. 'Last I saw of 'em they were up on the rimrock near the shack.'

'Doing what? They'd no reason to go there! Or mebbe you made them, so you could burn them?'

'No — nothing like that! All I burned was Rocky Campbell's corpse. I took the women with me so I could keep an eye on 'em. They'd come into town with the body, so we had to take precautions mighty quick.' Perspiring freely, Carl jerked his head away from the knife and then wished he had not because he had to keep it at that uncomfortable angle when the blade followed him.

'What precautions?' Neil barked, the knife immovable.

'That body had three slugs in it from my Colt. I didn't want Holton to examine it.'

'Because you shot Campbell when you knew he was the one living piece of evidence Syl wanted to clear me! Right?'

Carl gave a gasp and writhed as the point pressed sharply enough to draw a drop of blood.

'Yeah, yeah!' he shouted. 'That's right!' Carl sweated profusely and his eyes rolled as he felt pain down his spine from the unnatural angle of his neck.

'Rocky kidnapped Syl on your orders, didn't he?'

'Yeah, he did. For God's sake let me up! I can hardly breathe — '

'Too bad — we've more to discuss yet. How's about putting your head a bit further back, huh?' Neil pressed the blade point again and Carl was forced to put his head still further to one side. The slightest effort to relax brought him against the blade tip.

'That blacksmith pal of yours has confessed,' Neil continued relentlessly. 'I made him. All I need now is your own confession that you framed me just like you admitted it to Syl. You've half done it, so you might as well finish it. *Finish it*!' He jabbed the blade.

'Hold it! *Hold it!*' The sting in the side of his throat brought a rush of words from Carl. 'It's right! I did frame you to get even with you — and that redskin — but it won't do you any more good than it did Syl. You've no witnesses . . . '

'That's where you're wrong, Naylor!' The voice came from the doorway. 'All right, Neil, I'm satisfied,' Sheriff Holton added. 'On your feet, Naylor.'

Neil rose and flung the knife contemptuously into the table top where it swung gently on its point. Slowly Carl eased his excruciating neck muscles back into position, wiped the trickle of blood from his neck, then scrambled up. He stared fixedly at Sheriff Holton as he came forward, gun in hand.

'I get it,' Carl muttered venomously. 'A frame-up, to make me talk!'

'You should complain about frame-ups,' Holton said, with a hard smile. 'Better get movin', Naylor. With what you've admitted, and Ben's confession,

I've enough to ask for a retrial as far as Neil's concerned — and no doubt as to the verdict. We're riding back into town right now.'

Set-faced, Carl moved forward sullenly, the sheriff's gun following him. Then as he passed the table Carl whipped up the knife and flung it savagely straight for Holton's gunhand. Holton fired, his shot going wide, then he dropped his weapon as vivid red coursed over the top of his hand.

In a matter of seconds Carl had the gun, and aimed it steadily.

'You are the only two who know the facts, save perhaps Ma and Syl, but they won't talk in a hurry again, I reckon . . . '

He relaxed against the table, enjoying his mastery of the situation as the two men looked at him warily, Holton meanwhile wrapping his kerchief about his hand.

'Yeah,' Carl continued, grinning as he saw Neil's horrified expression. 'That blasted girl and your ma *are* dead! They weren't burned up, far as I know, but I did fix it for their cayuses to take a plunge over the rimrock into the gorge. Later on I aim to look for their bodies.'

Neil said nothing but his eyes flamed with fury. He took half a step forward but the levelled gun jerked up.

'With them gone and you two following right now, I shan't have much to worry about in future.' Carl grinned. 'Nobody will ever be able to prove anything. Any last words before I pull this trigger?'

Instead of an answer there came a sudden sound from the darkness of the hall. Carl glanced in its direction and swung his gun all in the same second.

He fired into darkness, but another shot came a fraction before his. Red welled suddenly on his white shirt across his heart and his gun dropped out of his hand just as Neil dived upon him. With a choking gasp Carl caught at the table edge, clung to it desperately, then fell with heavy vibration to the floor.

'For land's sakes, gal, you got him!' yelled a delighted voice from the hall. 'Right in the ticker! I never figured you'd be able to do it!'

'Ma! Syl!' Neil yelled, and dashed for the doorway just as his mother and the girl came through it. He stared at them, his expression alternating between delight and dismay. Sheriff Holton's jaw dropped, and his eyebrows went up in astonishment.

Both women were filthy dirty, their clothes scorched and in tatters, their front hair and eyebrows singed, whilst across their faces were blisters raised from savage heat.

'Syl!' Neil gasped, catching her in his arms as she swayed a little.

'I'm — I'm all right,' she whispered, as he settled her in a chair.

'What the hell's been happening to you?'

'Plenty!' Ma snapped, dogged as ever. 'That coyote Naylor ditched us up on the rimrock where the shack was — but we got free.' She explained briefly how Sylvia had obtained the knife and continued:

'After that we dragged out the body of Campbell before it got too burned up. It's in a helluva mess but there's enough of it for the bullets to be dug out, an' matched with Naylor's Colt. We had to wait until the fire was low enough for us to dump Campbell's body on one of the horses — which we were able to restrain from going over the edge — then we rode into town to look for you, Sheriff, and found you weren't around anywheres.'

'Guess Fleet and I must have just missed you,' Neil said, thinking.

'We was wonderin' what to do,' Ma continued, 'when Ben's old woman came out of their shack an' demanded to know if we'd seen her old man around. She said she'd heard your voice, Sheriff, an' hadn't seen her old man since.'

'Then what?' Holton asked, listening intently.

Ma shrugged. 'We figured Ben might

be in one of the cells back of your office, so we busted our way in. It was important to us to know if you'd arrested that blacksmith since he's a mighty powerful witness. We found him all right an' Fleet told me by signs that you and Neil had probably come over to the Leanin' L here. We busted open some drawers in the sheriff's office, tryin' to find a key to free Fleet, but we couldn't find anythin'. So we upped and rode on here ... ' She broke off with a grim chuckle. 'Damnedest thing was, we was both unarmed, but the gal here stood on a Colt as we came up the porch, and picked it up. Good bit of luck, that!'

'Not really, Ma, and certainly not for Naylor! I made him drop it outside there, when I arrived.'

'You mean he was shot with his *own* gun? Hot damn, that's a good 'un!' Ma smiled broadly, then gave a little shrug. 'Well, I reckon that's all. Campbell's corpse is on a cayuse outside an' you've gotten the blacksmith sewn up. Naylor got what was a-comin' to him a bit before his time, that's all. An' Neil can be in the clear from here on.'

'You're dead right he can, Ma,' Holton agreed, nursing his hand. Then the brief ensuing silence was broken by a plaintive wail from Sylvia.

'And look at me!' she complained, tears of fatigue starting into her eyes. 'My hair and eyebrows are ruined and I must look like nothing on earth — And I'm so *tired*! I could weep! In fact I *will* . . . .' And she did, thoroughly, tears streaming down her sooty and fire-blistered cheeks.

'OK, gal, weep — I reckon you've earned it,' Ma said, looking at her. 'Y' can ride like hell's own; you've got the courage of a mountain lioness when you're in a tight corner, an' dang me if you can't shoot straight with a forty-five, too! That bead you got on Naylor was a lulu! I'll never forget it! *Straight to the heart*! I'm proud of you, gal!'

'You — really are?' Sylvia asked,

hesitating, and her tears ceased.

'Coming from Ma Grantham I reckon that's a mighty big chunk of flattery,' Holton commented, grinning.

Sylvia licked her dry, damaged lips. She looked at Neil as he kneeled beside her. He tried not to smile at the unhappy mess she looked.

'I — I suppose I ought to go back home now,' she said miserably.

'Like hell you will!' Ma snorted. 'Not with what we've got packed away in a certain cavern! I aim to start livin' big an' git a bit of comfort out of life. Seems to me it's about time I did — and you two'll be included in it! Come to think of it, gal, we might make things pretty much like you'd been led to expect 'em. Big spread, four thousand head. Eh, Neil?'

'Uh-huh.' Neil grinned.

'What's all this about?' the sheriff asked. 'You come into money or somethin', Ma?'

'Never you mind,' Ma answered, with a dubious wink. 'You don't suppose I slaved all my life for nothin', do you?'

'I — I suppose I would find it dreadfully quiet back home after all that's happened here,' Sylvia said. 'I've done so much. Even stopped smoking, too!'

'Listen, Syl,' Neil drew her head towards his shoulder, 'I've always wanted you to stay, only you were that plain obstinate . . . '

'Why not?' she whispered. 'I had to be after the way you deceived me at first — but though I've never admitted it before I was really sort of pleased, because you'd taken such a risk just to make sure of getting me. It doesn't matter now, though. You won't want a girl like me — toughened, different from the girl you thought you were getting.'

'It's because you're different and so like the rest of us out here that I do want you.' Neil laughed. 'You're a real girl of the West! I want you even more than I ever did before!'

'But, Neil . . . ' Sylvia's lips quivered.

'I'm an awful sight. My hair — my face —'

'So what?' He laughed. 'The doc will fix those burns, and your hair will grow again. In a few weeks you'll be the same old Syl . . . if only you'll stay.'

'Not quite the same old Syl,' she said wearily, relaxing. 'I'll never be that again.'

Neil kissed her gently and then frowned as she took no notice.

'Don't let it worry you, son,' Ma told him, with a wink at the sheriff. 'It ain't that the gal doesn't want to kiss you back. She's that dead asleep I guess even an earthquake won't wake her.'

THE END